OPERATOR 5:
MARCH OF THE FLAME MARAUDERS

SECRET SERVICE #5™
OPERATOR 5
AMERICA'S UNDERCOVER ACE

MARCH OF THE FLAME MARAUDERS

By Curtis Steele

STEEGER BOOKS • 2020

CHAPTER 1
TORCH OF TERROR

B LACK POWER was flowing out of the black ground and through the open blackness of the night—a precious, odorous, slimy stuff draining from the veins of Mother Earth—crude oil.

The drumming throb of a giant pump beat through the air from the shadow of a gaunt tower. Panting machinery, driven by a pulsing Diesel engine, sucked the sticky petroleum from the depths of *El Oro Negro* well, shot it through thick pipelines and sent it in gushing viscidly into the maws of the greasy tank-cars on the railway spur. Hour after hour, day after day and night after night, the well-crew had been laboring without rest to capture every possible drop of this dark blood of the earth.

The wan light of the Texas moon faded into the electric glare surrounding the *Oro Negro,* and the blinding bulbs threw long, thin shadows of the moving men about the base of the tower. Their motions were quick and tense; their clothing, their skin, their lungs were permeated with the oil that made the atmosphere pungent—oil to be refined into fuel vitally needed by the defenses of the nation.

On the roads stretching away from the *Oro Negro,* other men, wearing the uniform of the United States infantry, stood on guard with ready rifles. They kept constantly alert, though none of the traffic on the highways turned toward the well

1

MARCH OF THE FLAME MARAUDERS

Sabotage! Countless oil
wells going up in flame;
more tankers sunk!

they guarded. For a week, they had been watching the strange exodus that was carrying hundreds from the boom-towns of the oil-field—that was leaving the villages lightless and empty and silent.

Tonight, the last of the few remaining families were deserting Rainbow Creek, the town which lay a few miles away, on the edge of the field. Wheezing cars, loaded with household goods, rattled past. The grimy faces of men and women and children peered into the glare of the *Oro Negro* as they turned their backs upon it.

Theirs were the hungry, despairing faces of those who had once earned their bread by oil—who were now facing a future as black as the sticky liquid which had failed them. Behind them, they were leaving Rainbow Creek deserted.

The town stood gaunt and lifeless, its modest homes abandoned, its stores stripped and locked, its offices emptied, its streets echoing no step. No window shone with a light. A few stray animals lurked in the darkness; but in all the town, there was no scrap of forage left. Upon the discovery of oil in that territory, Rainbow Creek had mushroomed into being, created by the black magic of petroleum; now it was doomed to molder into the dust of the sandy plain.

Into the silence of Rainbow Creek came the soft purr of an engine. The bright headlights of a sleek roadster shafted a white beam down the empty, main street. The glow of the dash shone into the alert, blue eyes and the clean-cut face of the young man at the wheel; into the freckled features of the alert-looking boy who sat beside him. In dismayed silence, they peered through bleak windows, into bare rooms, as they rolled toward the jungle of oil-towers ahead.

"A year ago, Tim," the young man at the wheel said quietly as he shot the roadster along the highway, "this field was the richest oil-reserve in the country. It was pouring out a vast store of petroleum. There are fifteen thousand wells in this section, and each one was producing countless barrels of crude oil every day. Now—"

HE PEERED into the forest of gaunt towers spreading all around—a bleak, deserted wilderness. Except for the gleam of the *Oro Negro,* it was as devoid of life as the town they had just passed through.

"Now," he continued, "there is only one well producing. All the others are exhausted. One after another, they began to give up salt water instead of oil. All the oil men, who rushed here when the boom broke, have taken their families away—because staying here would mean starvation. One of the richest natural resources of the United States has ceased to exist. What is infinitely worse, this scene is being duplicated in almost every oilfield in the country."

The grave-faced boy was studying, in the glow of the dash, the headlines of several newspapers which he had brought with him.

"We knew from the beginning," his companion continued solemnly, "that oil is an exhaustible natural product. A certain store of it was created beneath the crust of the earth in long-past ages; that store must sometime give out completely. We are facing that situation now, Tim—an extremely serious situation.

Most of our oil reserves have been consumed, and the supply we have left can't last long. When the last drop is gone—"

The young man's voice faded; his right hand strayed from the wheel to a golden ornament dangling on his watch-chain. The back of that hand bore a strange scar—a marking of black and white and gray shaped like a spread-winged American eagle. The charm with which his supple fingers toyed was quite as strange. It was an artfully contrived skull-and-crossbones, fashioned of finest gold. Its eyes were brilliant red rubies. Unconsciously, his gesture expressing the appalling thought that occupied him, the young man touched the symbol of death.

The boy peered again at the banner headlines of the newspapers. The dash-light shone upon a ring he wore. It pictured a white skull against a black background, and on its forehead the mystic numeral 5 was emblazoned. The boy's ring was strikingly similar to the watch-charm worn by his companion; it sparkled no less brightly than his eyes as he read the startling headlines:

> U.S. FACES GREAT OIL FAMINE! NATION'S
> RESERVES VANISHING!
> Crisis Endangers Country, Forcing Dras-
> tic Measures to Conserve Oil Stores!

"I didn't realize oil was so important!" the boy exclaimed. "I thought that our oil supplies would never give out!"

"Oil is as vital to us as food," the young man at the wheel

answered. "The welfare of the United States depends on it.* Our daily lives can't go on without it and our national defenses will be powerless. In a thousand odd ways, lack of sufficient oil will seriously handicap us. We've got to face the facts, Tim. This crisis is one of the worst that has ever threatened the United States, and unless we—"

"Stop your car!"

THE RINGING command shrilled through the smooth hum of the motor. A United States infantryman leaped into the shine of the headlights. The driver of the roadster quickly applied the brakes. A second uniformed man joined the first, and they approached, with rifles steadied. Their gleaming eyes shone with a forbidding light: "You can't go on unless you have a pass!"

"Perhaps," the young man at the wheel asked quietly, "this will do?"

He removed a thin, silver case from an inner pocket. A touch of his thumbnail on a hidden spring released a leaf, and disclosed

---

* AUTHOR'S NOTE: "The United States not only consumes more oil than any other country, but it is more dependent upon oil, with its oil-fueled navy, a merchant marine sixty-two percent oil-burning, and its 25,000,000 motor cars."—Leonard M. Fanning, Director of Publicity, American Petroleum Institute, New York.

a document inside. The infantrymen leaned to read the brief message and their eyes widened with surprise.

THE WHITE HOUSE
Washington

To Whom It May Concern:

The identity of the bearer of this letter must be kept strictly confidential.

He is Operator 5 of the United States Intelligence Service.

The signature affixed to the credential was that of the President of the United States.

"Certainly, sir!" one of the armed men exclaimed, stepping back. "Go ahead!"

James Christopher—designated in the secret archives of the United States Intelligence Service as Operator 5—peered into the glare of lights of the *Oro Negro* as he sped on. The pungency of the greasy air was sharper when he pulled to the side of the road. He slipped out and touched the light-switch; the head-lamps blinked twice, then once again, before they snapped out.

In the glare at the base of the tower, a dark figure began striding toward him. Operator 5 removed a yellow flimsy from his pocket and reread its message. It was an order from WDC-13—the central headquarters of the United States Intelligence in Washington—which had brought him to this exhausted oil-field:

... SPECIAL ATTENTION OPERATOR 5... A-9

STATIONED ORO NEGRO WELL RAINBOW CREEK TEXAS REPORTS SUSPICIOUS ACTIVITY AT NEARBY EXHAUSTED WELL… A-9 DOUBTS ACTIVITY CONNECTED WITH OIL PRODUCTION… SUSPECTS TESTING STATION OF SOME NEW WEAPON OF ATTACK… NO SUCH STATION KNOWN TO WAR DEPARTMENT… URGE YOUR ATTENTION AT ONCE… Z-7, WDC-13….

The shadowed man, who had approached from the well, paused and peered at Operator 5 intently. His coveralls were soaked with oil, his face was grimy, but his eyes were sharp and alert. He said in a whisper: "Crude still coming!"

"Production maintained?" Operator 5 inquired.

"Pressure dropping."

"Work tonight."

The man in the greasy coveralls glanced around alertly now that the signals were exchanged. "I've been expecting you, Operator 5," he said quietly. "I saw your signal with the lights. So far, thank God, we're safe!"

"You're sure of every man working at the well? You've checked them all thoroughly? If the production of the *Oro Negro* were lost now, it would be a staggering blow, A-9."

"I know! I've been on watch constantly. You're here because—?"

"That other well where the suspicious activity is going on— where is it?" Operator 5 asked quietly. "I'm very interested in that. I know that secret agents of other nations, all vitally concerned with oil—Great Britain, Russia and Japan, among others—are at work even now in this country. It's very possible that the *Oro Negro* can be destroyed by some power striking underground at it. Every precaution must—"

OPERATOR 5 broke off as a sharp cry rang from a man at the base of the tower: "Look out! Get away! It's going up!"

"Fire!"

"Fire!"

Flaring light sprang out of the shadows of the *Oro Negro* as the terrorized shout carried its warning. Operator 5 whipped about, saw flames leaping high on the oil-soaked ground near the main pipe-line—scarlet, roaring flames plumed with black! Through the glare, men were running with desperate speed. Swiftly, as the gleam sparkled in Jimmy Christopher's dismayed eyes, the fire flooded outward from its source—a spreading tide of flames that snarled with hot, savage power as it leaped up the gaunt tower.

"Get away!" a scream sounded. "We can't stop it!"

"Back the cars!"

"Stop the pump!"

"Clear away!"

Operator 5 stepped back swiftly, gripping A-9's greasy arm, snapping a command at the wide-eyed boy. "Into the car! Quick, Tim!"

He leaped to the wheel as the roaring flames licked high into the sky, paling the moon, blotting over the stars, pouring out a choking, black cloud. As the Diesel engine of the road-ster whirred into action, the shadowed men nearer the base of the burning well sped to other cars. Starters rasped, engines surged, men yelled in terrorized dismay. On the spur, the string of tank-cars clashed as the locomotive began a hasty retreat from the withering furnace. Jimmy Christopher swung his roadster sharply, speeding it toward the highway beyond.

A-9 gasped: "It's an accident! Nobody could have set that fire! Nobody's been near—!"

Explosion!

The terrific concussion tore the night with fire that streamed into the zenith and burst in a blasting cloud over all the surrounding earth. A thundering ball of flame swelled, spewing black earth that burned as it flew, rocking the foundations of the world. Over the whole sky, the flame blasted, white-hearted, rolling off black fumes. With the cosmic power of lightning, the explosion struck doom to the precious *Oro Negro*.

The force drove down upon Operator 5's roadster, rolling a blinding cloud of flame around it. Deadly heat engulfed the three in the car as Jimmy Christopher ducked low and jammed the accelerator to its limit. One instant, all of creation was in flames; one instant, and the burst receded, leaving the soaked ground fuming and flaming in spots. Smoke trailed the blistered roadster as echoes rumbled back from the depths of the night—as the surrounding land flickered with the red glare of destruction.

Operator 5 peered back in horror at the huge torch flaring high into the sky. The tower of the *Oro Negro* had been toppled by the blast; now, twisted, broken, it was already glowing red-hot in the terrific heat of the inferno. The flames were gushing from the red maw of a crater torn into the earth. Broken pipe-lines were pouring out fire. The string of tank-cars was enveloped in roaring red along its entire length. And the light of the terrific conflagration showed where death had struck.

The bodies of men lay flaming on the ground. Cars bathed in fire were still rolling forward while cries of agonized torture tore from the lips of the men trapped in them. Across the fuming terrain other cars were speeding, their tops blazing. The powerful concussion had tossed several machines aside and they lay near the red holocaust—biers for the men who had not lived to escape. The night glared red with the color of terror and death....

JIMMY CHRISTOPHER raced along the highway, out of the area stricken by the blast. He swerved to the side of the road and stopped while A-9 scrambled out, stunned. The tough Irish lad peered with Operator 5 across land shrouded in fumes, lighted by a high-reaching torch. The ground rumbled as though the power of the flames had penetrated beneath the earth's crust, fed by air sucked down the cores of other wells opening into the same cavern. The black gold of the well had been transformed into black doom!

Secret Agent A-9 was peering at Jimmy Christopher in horror. "An accident must have started it!" he gasped again. "A spark struck somehow! No man in that crew would have set it!"

"Perhaps no man in the crew set that fire," Jimmy Christopher yelled through the roar, "but it was no accident. That fire was started deliberately, to destroy the *Oro Negro!*"

"But how is that possible?" A-9 demanded breathlessly. "I checked every man who's been near the well! I watched them all. I tell you, no one could have slipped past the guards and started that fire!"

"You did your best, A-9—I'm sure of that," Operator 5 replied. "No one stole past you to set that fire. I may be wrong, but it must have been done in a way you couldn't possibly have detected—in a way that a hundred men couldn't have stopped."

The light of the fire was nickering in his eyes, and they had grown dangerously dark. "The destruction of that well means sabotage—forces working undercover against us. It means that there is a force striving to bring the United States to her knees—striving to crush her with the black power of oil!"

A-9 peered appalled into Jimmy Christopher's dark-lined face. Tim Donovan gazed stunned into his eyes. His gaze did not turn to either of them. Operator 5 stood motionless, looking into the white-hot heart of the gigantic torch flaring high into the sky. His fingers were toying with the golden death-charm on his watch chain, and the red of its eyes was glittering bright....

Jimmy Christopher turned briskly. "Into the car!" he commanded. "A-9, we're going directly to the other well you spotted. We've no time to lose!"

"Straight ahead!"

The Diesel engine of the roadster—fueled by the same black substance which was now consuming itself where the famed

Oro Negro had stood—sang its song of power as Operator 5 sent it streaking over the road. Tim Donovan pulled his cap tight against the rush of the wind; A-9 peered back haggardly at the blaze as skeleton towers flicked past.

"God! All that oil going up in smoke when it's needed desperately by our navy and air corps!" he exclaimed. "A year ago, the loss of one well would have meant nothing—but now it's a major disaster!"

Operator 5's lips pressed tightly as he nodded. "The United States has been too slow to realize the vital value of our oil," he declared. "We have been blind to the truth while other nations have realized its importance fully. Now we're paying dearly for our short sightedness. We've squandered our oil, and permitted it to be squandered for us, and now the end of our reserve is in sight."

Tim Donovan exclaimed: "Gee, Jimmy, I remember your talking about oil a year ago—saying that we were heading into danger—but nobody would listen to you. Everybody seemed to think our oil would last forever and we didn't need to worry about it."

OPERATOR 5 smiled wryly. "I wasn't alone in that Tim. Scientists have warned us repeatedly that our oil was certain to become depleted soon—but there are a dozen reasons why nothing was done about it. Commercial greed, crooked gangs, politics—they all kept on draining our reserves. And while we were doing nothing, other nations were acting.

"Every other great power in the world began to assure itself of an oil reserve many years ago. Ever since the first World War, there has been a secret struggle going on between nations—a secret fight to control as much of the world's oil supply as possible. The people in general have known nothing about it. But it has been a life-and-death conflict, taking place undercover, and the fate of every nation has been hanging in the balance."

"Has the United States been getting the worst of it, Jimmy?" Tim Donovan asked anxiously. "We've let ourselves get into a bad fix?"

"Such a bad fix, Tim," Jimmy Christopher answered, "that very soon we will certainly find ourselves fighting with our backs to the wall."

A-9 peered intently into Operator 5's set face. "Thank God you're on this case!" he exclaimed. "You'll be able to help us, if no one else can, to save the little oil we have left!"

Jimmy Christopher's eyelids lowered. "No one man," he declared levelly, "nor one million men, will be able to save the United States from complete destruction if we find ourselves totally without oil."

A-9 stared. "What? Is it possible—do you believe it possible that—?"

"The situation in which we find ourselves makes any disaster possible!"

Operator 5's grim declaration struck A-9 and Tim Donovan silent. They gazed into his gleaming eyes as though striving to read the secret fear that lay behind his words, but his face was a baffling mask. He kept the roadster speeding ahead and did not glance aside until A-9 suddenly declared:

"It's right ahead! Don't go too close! The place is probably guarded. I warn you—going near that place may be dangerous!"

Operator 5 swung the roadster across the side of the road and rolled it slowly over oily ground. They had reached the edge of the oil-field; here, the towers were fewer. The one which A-9 indicated rose alone in the midst of a spreading open space. Jimmy Christopher switched out his headlamps, drove warily toward a high steel fence which enclosed the well. He braked and peered at the black shell of the structure sitting in the shadow of the tower.

A-9 explained as they left the car: "There's a pipeline running from that well to the next, outside the fence. I can't tell you what it means, because both wells were among the first to become exhausted in this field. The layout has stumped me."

"I intend to find out exactly what it means," Jimmy Christopher declared quietly.

THREE VAGUE figures, moving silently, they crossed the blackish ground. Far beyond the horizon, a red shine lighted the sky—the glare of the fire at the *Oro Negro*. The roar of the conflagration carried on the wind; flames licked into sight occasionally, even at this distance. When Operator 5 paused, he was at the door of a shack located beneath the rearing oil-tower that sat behind the fenced section.

He listened to be sure no one was inside; he stepped through quietly. Tim Donovan stood at his side as his electric torch played its circle upon the thick pipe angling down into the ground. A-9 bent beside him as he listened. From beneath the surface of the ground came a dull, rushing sound, constant in its pitch—an earthy whisper. Jimmy Christopher rose, stepped to a thinner pipe protruding a few feet away. He held his hand above its open end.

"Air rushing out," he declared. "That's strange. No oil is being taken from this well, of course—but oil is being poured into it."

A-9 blurted: "Impossible! Where could the oil be coming from, if that were true? This large pipe leads directly to the other well, inside the fence, and that one gave out months ago. And why should anyone deliberately pump oil back into the earth?"

Again Operator 5 murmured: "Strange…! The other well may have gone dry months ago, A-9, but it is producing now. Thousands of barrels of petroleum are passing from the other well to this one—oil that our navy and army are starving for. This is nothing as simple as a case of 'hot oil.'* It's far more than that—far more!"

---

* AUTHOR'S NOTE: "Hot oil"—oil illegally produced in spite of conservation measures—was, late last year, flowing at the rate of 125,000 barrels a day out of the East Texas field, a strip of land thirty-six miles long and six miles wide, where lay the richest pool of oil ever discovered by man. Six years ago, small farmers were plowing sandy fields and producing meager crops there—until Dad Joiner, an old-fashioned wild-cat driller, digging into ground where oil geologists declared there was no oil, drilled to a depth of 3,600 feet and produced a well yielding 15,000 barrels a day without effort. In four years 14,000 wells were put down into that field. Here the government attempted to conserve the invaluable and rapidly diminishing supply, and here "hot oil" flowed in illegal defiance of the government regulations, which strove to reduce the production per well from 15,000 barrels daily to

"I don't understand, Operator 5!"

Jimmy Christopher peered at A-9. "Listen!" he declared briskly. "Take my roadster and head immediately for the nearest telegraph station. Wire Z-7 at WDC-13 your report on the *Oro Negro*. Warn him that our vigilance against sabotage must be doubled at all points. Our men must be warned to look particularly for Scheele detonators. Return here immediately. I'm going to take a look, meantime, at that other well."

"What! Alone?" A-9 blurted. "With only this boy to—"

"Tim Donovan," Operator 5 interrupted smiling, "is not a member of the Intelligence for one reason only—his age. I consider him the equal of any man in the service. The orders I just gave you are very important."

"Yes, sir!"

JIMMY CHRISTOPHER'S torch blinked out. He stepped from the shack, watched A-9 hurry through the dim shine of the moon toward the roadster. He waited motionless until a murmur in the air told him that the secret agent was speeding off. He peered past the high mesh fence, at the black building beyond, and spoke quietly:

"On your toes, old-timer. The devil only knows what we're

---

40 barrels. Similarly, illegal oil was being drained from all other reserves in the country. Hot oil flows through secret pipes, out of dummy wells, into smuggling tanks, through fake refineries, in a hundred different ways to deceive the federal agents—draining the most precious oil reservoirs within the boundaries of the United States.

heading into. There's oil flowing through that pipe—the only oil in all this field now—and I'm going to find out why."

"Oil flowing back into the ground, Jimmy, while our Atlantic fleet is being called back from maneuvers because of shortage of oil?"

"Exactly! Watch sharp, Tim!"

Operator 5 moved silently toward the stout, mesh fence. Tim Donovan drifted at his side. They turned when they reached the steel barrier. Near a gate Jimmy Christopher paused, cautiously inspecting it without touching it. It was fastened by a padlock and a chain passing around the two posts. From his pocket, Operator 5 removed his pack of master keys—implements of his own devising, capable of opening any known type of lock—and listened.

"Someone is inside that shack," he whispered, stepping forward. "Machinery is working. Keep your gun handy, Tim!"

Three times he fitted a key into the padlock before the hasp clicked. He loosened the chain and straightened warily. Bit by bit, he swung the gate wide. It moved without sound; no alarm came from the shack. Operator 5 stepped forward—and suddenly he leaped!

All the strength of his supple, snapping muscles hurled him backward through the gate. At the same time, a sharp, metallic click sounded.

Tim Donovan, whirling aside, saw Operator 5 squirm in mid-air, sprawl to the ground. The breathless boy darted forward. Jimmy Christopher kneed up while a chain rattled on the ground. Together they peered at a heavy, steel trap which had fastened its toothed jaws on Operator 5's shoe.

"A bear trap!" Jimmy Christopher had felt the dirt give way almost imperceptibly beneath his foot as he was stepping through the gate. His weight had released the trigger of the trap buried in the ground. Only his swift leap had saved him from the jagged teeth, had kept the powerful springs from crushing the sharp jaws upon his leg. The heel of his shoe had been caught; the steel points were buried in the leather. The chain, linked to the trap and banded to a stake driven deep in the earth, pinioned him now.

"Careful, Tim!" he warned in a whisper. "There may be other traps buried around the gate! If one gets you, it will break your leg—and it's impossible to get out of one of them without a special spring-clamp!"

The boy stood with caught breath as Operator 5 peered at the dark shack with leveled automatic. There was no movement in the shadows; no sound. Jimmy Christopher stooped, gripped the huge trap and twisted it; he tore two lifts from the heel of his shoe and freed himself. Grimly he brought his torch into his hand, and his finger poised on the button.

"Whoever is in that shack protects himself well, Tim!" he whispered. "Stick close behind me. I'll go ahead."

He pressed the button of his torch. A single instant, a circle of light gleamed on the ground. Operator 5 carried the trap through the gate, placed it aside; Tim Donovan closed the way.

21

Again the light glared and disappeared as they eased ahead. Each step a separate—danger, Jimmy Christopher moved tight-muscled toward the oil-blackened shack.

THE RHYTHMIC noise of machinery working inside became louder. A hissing sound came and went. Rounding the corner, Operator 5 saw that an extension had been built to the shack recently—a structure without windows. In one wall stood a door. Jimmy Christopher's light blinked to the ground again as he approached it.

He slipped along the wall, avoiding the path. He paused when he sensed a movement inside. After a moment of silence, he pressed on. He whipped gloves from his pocket when he noted that the knob was metal, and drew them on. Operator 5 had learned in the past how efficiently a high-potential electric current could function as guard; he was determined to avoid every possible trap. His covered hand reached to the knob, twisted—and jerked back!

Steel lightninged in the gloom. With dazzling swiftness, a small aperture had appeared in the door—the long, keen blade of a sword had jabbed outward through it! Jimmy Christopher's tense recoil twisted him aside as the gleaming point drove toward him. It snagged into the cloth of his coat—it pierced! The shining steel ran close to his skin, ripping out behind his arm. He stood motionless, breath locked in his lungs, the sword skewered through his clothing, its coldness chilling his heart.

For a moment, the blade did not move. Operator 5 was forced to remain rigid while Tim Donovan stared appalled. He knew that someone on the inside of the door must be gripping the hilt of the sword, that any movement he made would send a warning tremor inward. The razor-edged steel, except for Operator 5's swift whirl away, would have pierced his body below the heart. Now, every muscle tight, he waited.

Inside, a low voice sounded: "Orth! What is it, Orth?"

Nearer the door—from the man who had thrust the sword outward—the answer came: "I thought I heard somebody. I thought I saw the knob twist—but the sword didn't hit!"

"Make sure!"

The steel blade gleamed anew, began to withdraw. It slid back through the gashes it had cut in Operator 5's coat. The instant he was freed, Jimmy Christopher whirled aside, gesturing Tim behind him. The knob of the door rattled. A line of light widened from a crack. The elongated shadow of a man appeared, his one hand gripping the sword. He stepped outward cautiously—and Jimmy Christopher struck!

At his step, the man with the sword spun to face him. The blade slashed upward. Operator 5 drove a swift blow to the man's forehead. His stiff fingers sharply struck and twisted. A breathy gasp sounded; the man with the sword went stiff. Unbending as a stone statue, he toppled. Operator 5 stepped in again and caught him. He dragged the man with the sword into the shadow. He straightened coldly, confident that his jiu-jitsu blow would keep his assailant unconscious for at least an hour. Then he turned to face the door.

Silent steps carried him inward. He passed through a small, dark room with Tim Donovan following, wide-eyed. He thrust a door open, strode into blindingly bright light. His automatic gleamed at a bearded man in a greasy smock who was bending to peer at the gleaming face of a giant gauge. Jimmy Christopher's command rang sharply: "Don't move!"

CHAPTER 2
BLACK MENACE

G LITTERING EYES jerked toward Jimmy Christopher—eyes wide-opened, peering through thick-lensed spectacles. The face of the man at the gauge went white. He turned slowly, stood motionless—a stocky figure enveloped in an oil-stained smock, his hard-pressed lips almost hidden by his bushy beard and mustache; his gaze a defiance. He blurted breathily: "Who are you?"

Operator 5 answered: "My name does not matter. It is enough for you to know that I am an agent of the United States government. I want to know exactly what you're doing here."

The man in the smock glared angrily. "You have no right to break in! I own this tract and every well within a mile. The surface and the sub-surface rights are completely mine—legally mine.* The United States government cannot touch me!"

"You are pumping oil out of this well and into the next,"

---

* AUTHOR'S NOTE: The United States is the only nation on earth in which the sub-surface rights of surface owners are not the government's prerogative. In all other nations, production of oil can be and is controlled by the government. The United States' attempts to conserve her oil reserves have met with failure.

Operator 5 declared levelly. "The United States is vitally concerned with every drop of oil available— with the use of it and the destruction of it. What do you know about the explosion of the *Oro Negro* a few minutes ago?"

"Nothing! Absolutely nothing!"

Jimmy Christopher looked his disbelief. "Unless you explain who you are, and why you are pumping thousands of barrels of precious oil back into the earth, I shall place you under arrest. You will make it easier for yourself if you speak now."

The man in the smock continued to glower defiantly. During a moment of silence, Jimmy Christopher's eyes darted about the room. From beyond came the constant beat and vibration of a tremendous pump which was sucking black, liquid gold out of the heart of the earth. To the walls, panels were affixed bearing numerous gauges, their needles nickering under fluctuating pressure. Here another pump was throbbing and hissing, and the thin pipes leading from it were trembling with imprisoned power. In the next room, through an open doorway, Operator 5 glimpsed row after row of scarred compressor tanks. Here were instruments and machinery not associated with the normal production of oil—equipment secretly installed and now performing a mysterious task.

The man in the smock blurted suddenly: "You will learn nothing from me! Nothing!"

"You are a citizen of the United States?"

"I hate your government!"

Again silence—except for the pulsing of the machinery, the hissing of compressed gas. Operator 5 studied the swarthy, bearded face of the man in the smock, looked into eyes blazing with hatred.

"You understand," Jimmy Christopher said quietly, "that the United States is face to face with a grave emergency. Hour by hour, our oil supply is decreasing. Our defenses are starving for the fuel you are pumping back into the ground. This will force us to confiscate your property and equipment."

" 'Confiscate—!' " The bearded man trembled with rage. "Your government was warned years ago that this danger would arise! The exhaustibility of oil was never a secret! Your government can blame no one for this emergency but itself!"*

"True," Jimmy Christopher admitted. "Because of that, we

---

* Author's Note: One of the most startling statements concerning the international struggle for oil is the following, by Sir Edwin Mackay Edgar, a London banker:

"While America is exhausting her supplies at a prodigal speed, we are getting a firmer grip on the world's oil reserves.

"I should say that two-thirds of the improved oil fields of Central and South America are in British hands.

"Or take again that greatest of all organizations, the Shell group. It owns exclusively or controls interests in every important oil-field in the world, including the United States, Russia, Mexico, the Dutch East Indies, Rouma-

are forced to desperate measures. We must have oil! Unless we assure ourselves of a new supply, we are lost!"

THE SMOCKED man's lips curled. "You need not tell me that. I have devoted my life to oil geology. I know more about petroleum supply and conservation than any other man living. I know how the nations of the world have fought to control the oil reserves of the world—at the cost of thousands of innocent lives; at the cost of untold suffering. Nature gave man oil as a blessing and man has turned it into a curse. I detest the merciless selfishness and the heartless greed that lie behind the struggle for oil!"

Operator 5 stepped slowly toward the bearded man, studying the face working with wrath, the eyes kindled with fanatical hatred.

"I will not add to the tragedy that has already come out of the secret war for oil!" the man in the smock burst out. "I will not

nia, Egypt, Venezuela, Trinidad, India, Ceylon, the Malay states, North and South China, Siam, the Straits Settlements, and the Philippines....

"We shall have to wait a few years before the full advantages of this situation shall begin to be reaped; but that the harvest will eventually be a great one there can be no manner of doubt.

"To the sum of many millions of pounds a year, America before long will have to purchase from British companies ... the oil she cannot do without and is no longer able to furnish from her own store.

"This is no revelation. The United States experts have been well aware of this situation for more than a year. But Congress and public opinion were not on their guard.... Unfortunately for them—and fortunately for us—their eyes have been opened too late."

make myself a pawn of any imperial nation! Let them destroy themselves as God wills!"

Jimmy Christopher's lips curved tightly. "You know, then, the danger threatening the United States? You have succeeded in drawing oil from a well which was abandoned as exhausted. Every drop of that oil is more precious than gold to us at this moment. Do you refuse to sell it to the government?"

"I refuse!"

"Even though you know that other nations have conspired to drain our oil supplies—have deliberately contrived to place the United States at their mercy*—you decline?"

"I refuse!"

---

* AUTHOR'S NOTE: From the oil reservoirs of the United States have been drained three-quarters of the world's oil *production!* Yet the oil *supply* of the United States was less than one-tenth that of the entire world! Of all the world's *production*, seven-tenths have been coming from the United States' smaller supply and only three-tenths from the huger supply of the rest of the world. It was long ago an inevitable conclusion that the oil supply of the United States, due to this disproportional production, would be drained long before the oil supplies of the rest of the world. And most startling of all is the belief that foreign oil competitors have actively conspired to hasten the process of draining the oil reserves of the U.S., in order to place this government at the mercy of others.

Refineries owned by a British company are located in New Orleans, Wood River, East Chicago, St. Louis, Wilmington and California. The same company has built a vast web of pipelines from which oil flows to Canada and abroad. The profits of the American subsidiaries of the British trust go

"In that case," Operator 5 declared grimly, "we are forced—"

"Jimmy!"

The whispered warning came from Tim Donovan. The boy was standing alert in the doorway behind Operator 5, listening. The machinery wheezed; the shack trembled; and the Irish lad moved quickly to Jimmy Christopher's side.

"Somebody's coming!" he exclaimed. "A car just stopped outside the fence!"

Jimmy Christopher saw alarm shine in the eyes of the man in the smock. The visitor, he realized, was not expected. He stepped aside alertly as a bell jangled inside the room—a signal from the gate. It rang three times, then twice, then three times again. The bearded man blinked in consternation while Operator 5 retreated, gun leveled, to the door of the adjoining shack.

"You know that signal," he said quietly, "but you do not

abroad, of course—and, it is claimed, are used to combat American competition in foreign fields!

Even more appalling is the fact that this British trust actually sold to Japan oil drained from a United States Naval reserve! Naval Reserve No. 2, located near the Elks Hill reserve in California, was held under lease by the Honolulu Oil Company which sub-leased the supply to Standard Oil of New Jersey. Upon the termination of their sub-lease, Standard discovered that Honolulu Oil had already negotiated a lease with the British trust. The British company immediately shipped the oil from the United States Naval reserve to its subsidiary in Japan—and this subsidiary held a contract to supply oil to the Japanese Navy—a huge oil-burning fleet which menaces the United States in the Pacific!

know who has rung it.
I am going to keep you
covered. Admit the man
at the gate. If you make
any unwise move—if
you betray my presence
here—you will have
cause to regret it."

The signal rang again. The angry color of the smocked man's face faded into whiteness. Jimmy Christopher backed through the opened door, into the gloomy space within which the giant pump was laboring. His automatic gleamed through the crack as he closed the door nearly shut.

"Let him in!" he commanded.

His keen gaze followed the bearded man across the room to the entrance. His touch on Tim Donovan's arm brought the boy close. He whispered quickly:

"Slip out, Tim! Watch that car! If anything happens here—trace it if possible and report to Z-7!"

"Sure, Jimmy, but—leaving you alone when—"

"Hurry it, Tim!"

OPERATOR 5 continued to peer through the crack, into the brightly lighted room, as the boy turned away. Tim Donovan drew the bolt of a stout door standing between two tar-papered windows. He slipped out into the dim shine of the moon and the door of the shack closed behind him. At the same moment, the bearded man opened the front entrance and a heavy voice spoke: "I have come here on extremely urgent business!"

"Who are you?" the voice of the man in the smock answered. "I do not know you."

"Allow me to enter and I will disclose my identity."

Operator 5 saw the bearded man retreat from the door. Into the room stepped a lean man, with box shoulders and a narrow face, his eyes a sharp, glittering gray. He strode into the light, glanced around alertly. His gaze lingered on the darkness in which Operator 5 was crouching; and he demanded: "Are we alone?"

"Yes, yes! Who are you? Where did you learn the signal? It was known only to—"

"We have means of learning things," the lean-faced man answered. "It was known only to your assistant Orth—yes. This, professor, will establish my identity."

The bearded man peered at a document which the other unfolded before his eyes. He frowned darkly. His wary visitor said softly:

"You understand now that I am Operator L-8 of the United States Intelligence-Service?"

"What do you want?"

"I am prepared to offer you the sum of five million dollars for the exclusive rights to your process."

The bearded man stiffened. "My process is not for sale!"

"Five million dollars, in a lump sum, at once!"

"There is not enough money in the world to buy my process! The United States shall never—!"

"If you persist in your refusal to accept this offer, I am under instructions to see that your secret remains unknown to all other nations of the world also."

The voice of the man, who had identified himself as L-8 of the United States Intelligence, grew sharp-edged. The professor retreated a step. He demanded falteringly: "What—what do you mean?"

"You have your choice, sir, between five million dollars—and *death!*"

The bearded man glanced around frantically. The other advanced threateningly toward him, gray eyes, glittering with an icy light. From the gloom, Operator 5 watched intently, automatic steadied.

"You will decide now—this instant!"

"I think not!" Operator 5's swift move carried him through the door as he snapped the words. The sound of his step, the ring of his words, jerked the lean man around. The glitter of his automatic checked the other's hand as it started to dart weapon-ward. Jimmy Christopher stood, gun steadied, peering into dangerous gray eyes.

"Lower your hand," he said quietly. "The alternative is exactly the same as that you just offered your host—death!"

The thin hand of the gray-eyed man dropped. Jimmy Christopher glimpsed, through the corners of his eyes, the bearded man retreating fearfully to the wall. He spoke, almost in a whisper:

"This man has presented himself to you, professor, as Operator L-8 of the United States Intelligence Service. He has lied. His credentials are forged. He is not acting for the government."

Jimmy Christopher's lips twirked tightly at the corners as the lean man started.

"He is, instead," Operator 5 continued, addressing the professor, "Jaime Coronza, a Spaniard, one of the most unscrupulous and dangerous international spies who ever lived!"

THE MAN in the smock backed to the wall beside the panel of gauges, his eyes widened in terror—his one trembling hand slowly raising.

"I am happy to encounter you, Señor Coronza," Jimmy Christopher asserted quietly. "I have known that you were in this country, engaging in destructive espionage activities against the United States. You will consider yourself my—"

Suddenly the man in the smock whirled; suddenly his hands darted high, gripped the handle of a lever protruding from the wall, swung it downward. Instantly a choking sound filled the room; black liquid flowed down the walls. From open vents crude oil began to pour. At the same moment, a spiteful crackling sound came; blue, electric light flashed.

The scientist's quick move spun Operator 5 to one side "Stand still, Coronza!" He snapped the warning and reached toward the lever on the wall. Cold air gushed; rusty hinges rasped, and he spun back again. Through a closing door at the rear of the room, he saw the hate-twisted face of the man in the smock—and the glitter of a revolver!

A swift shot! Operator 5 darted aside as the bullet spatted into the oil-drenched wall behind him. A second report rocked through the throbbing of the machinery and his own automatic blasted an echo. Jaime Coronza had snapped a weapon into his swarthy hand; it was yawning full toward Operator 5. It spat. And as Jimmy Christopher's gun answered a bursting concussion shook the room.

Flame gushed from the walls. Black smoke clouded to dim the incandescents. On both sides of Operator 5, in front of him and behind him, the walls became sheeted with flame. Blinding light stung his eyes; suffocating heat engulfed him instantly. Through the sudden roar, another shot cracked from Jaime Coronza's gun as Operator 5 leaped from flames licking at him from behind.

Coronza whirled to the entrance, kicked frantically at the flaming door as Jimmy Christopher sprang to follow. At his first move, a gun blasted again behind him. Bullets threatened from two directions—from Coronza and from the bearded man still peering through the door at the rear. With a gasp, Jimmy Christopher spun aside, blocked from any possible shelter by the withering flames that had spread over every inch of wall.

Black destruction was pouring thickly from the vents in the ceiling. Below them, between pointed wires, hot blue sparks were leaping. The lever the bearded man had moved opened the oil-pipes and closed a contact to operate spark-coils. Leaping, blue fire had ignited the pouring petroleum. Precious oil, streaming from a tank above the shack, had become a horrible trap of flame!

Operator 5 leaped to the door in the rear, twisting to slam a bullet at Coronza. The Spaniard slapped the door shut from the far side. Through the roar of the flames, his quick footfalls thudded. Jimmy Christopher grasped up a chair, charged at the rear door as it thumped shut. The panels resisted his blow as oil spread to cover them. A bolt rasped into the socket, shutting off the way the bearded man had gone.

Scorching air beat into Jimmy Christopher's lungs as he retreated. All around him, flaming oil continued to flow. Flames were trickling across the floor, forming a roaring pool. The air was blackening with unbreathable fumes. Operator 5 slapped his gun into its holster, slammed the chair at the flaming door connecting with the room beyond. He darted through—and found that room a snarling, blinding furnace.

SWIFTLY HE grasped one of the heavy compressor-tanks, tilted it, lugged it into his arms. He staggered toward the door through which the bearded man had gone. With all the strength he could summon, he drove the pointed end of the tank against the panels. Withering heat beat upon him. Oil dripped upon the tank, blazing. Behind him, the pool of flame was spreading—reaching fiery fingers toward him. Again and again, muscles straining, he crashed the heavy tank against the door.

The panels cracked and the freshly exposed wood caught fire. Flaming splinters dropped. The door crushed inward. Operator 5 dropped the tank, shielded his head with his arms, and sprang forward. His bound carried him through the door as oil dripped upon him. He whirled into darkness that flickered with the light of flames licking over his clothing—and found himself in an underground, dirt-floored tunnel.

Swiftly he snatched off his coat. Fire flared over it as he flung it away. He sped down an earthen slope, dug his shoes into loose dirt to smother the blazing oil he had tracked with him; he whipped frantically at the spots burning on his trousers. Gasping in the cold, damp air, he brought his automatic into his hand, peered along the depths of a passage lighted by the rising blaze behind him.

The roar of the conflagration drummed into the freshly dug tunnel. Rivulets of flame poured over the sill of the broken door, carrying creeping destruction down the slope as Jimmy Christopher plunged along it again. He knew that flames would soon flood the passage. He darted through rushing air that was feeding the fire, following fresh foot-tracks in the soft earth. He noted that the slope of the tunnel was rising—ahead he saw the faint gleam of moonlight.

A drumming roar beat in his ears as he charged into the open night. His swift glance around showed him a spreading, black field flickering with the light of the flaming buildings he had just escaped. Far across it, the gleam disclosed a winged form perching on the ground. A propeller was glistening in the glare; above the pit of the aircraft, weird vanes drooped. An autogyro—rolling, even as Operator 5 broke into a run, to the take-off!

In the pit of the gyro, the bearded man was crouched. His glittering revolver spat. A slug passed with a waspish whine near Operator 5's head. The open-throttled motor snarled its power as the strange craft gained speed. Jimmy Christopher aimed

Above him, the gyro droned, lifting through the glare of the flaming building!

37

with quick, grim care; he sent a single bullet toward the man in the pit. A scream of agony and fury mixed into the thunder of the motor—and the gyro leaped upward.

Jimmy Christopher sped to the spot as the craft rose sharply. A glitter on the ground attracted his attention. He saw a revolver lying in greasy grass—the gun his bullet had knocked from the bearded man's hand. He covered his fingers with a handkerchief; thrust the gun into his pocket. Above him, the gyro droned, whipping through the glare of the flaming buildings.

Operator 5 raced back. The flames were gushing up through cracked windows now, leaping the height of the tower. Flooding fire was pouring over the ground. Jimmy Christopher circled the roaring structure swiftly, while terrific heat beat upon him. He swung to the road, and paused in consternation, seeing that there was now no car near the gate. Jaime Coronza had reached his auto and fled. Through the snarling fire, Operator 5 called: "Tim! Tim!"

He heard no answer through the rumble shaking the earth. He darted to the gate from the side, to avoid more buried traps; he sped to the road. The thunder in the ground was taking on a more ominous tone each second. The light of the inferno spread far into the night, throwing a writhing shadow ahead of Jimmy Christopher as he ran. Beneath his feet, the ground shook, and swiftly—

A bursting shock struck through the flaming buildings. Terrific power burst the walls outward and they flew high and far, streaking, searing fragments. Earth spewed upward, carrying the blaze to scattered patches of soaked ground. The explosion tore pipe-sections from the ground, and a fountain of red flared high. From the one tower to the second the blaze leaped, and a snarling, mounting fury ripped out of the ground.

The power of the concussion struck Operator 5 as he ran. It hurled him forward through fire-filled air. It spilled him into choking, rolling fumes—black vapor that blanketed away even the glare of the roaring flames. It threw him into a darkness even deeper. Slumped motionless beside the road, amid whipping patches of flame, he lay unconscious....

High in the sky, the mechanical bat soared, the light of the flames glistening on its wings. Higher, into the reaches of the zenith where even the shine of the two giant torches did not penetrate. Higher still, till it vanished in the night....

CHAPTER 3
WARNING BY AIR

THE KNICKERBOCKER THEATRE stood apparently deserted, a few steps from the glaring, humming street called Broadway. The New York dramatic season had brought no sprightly production to its doors. Its marquee was sooted, its facade begrimed and lightless. Yet it was neither deserted nor empty. Hidden from all passersby, it bustled with tense, secret activity.

It was, unknown to the millions who thronged nearby that night, undercover Headquarters KT of the United States Intelligence Service. Sentinels guarded its doors, admitting quiet-mannered men who spoke a cryptic password. Behind its lowered curtain, on the wide stage shirt-sleeved workers bent over littered desks. In the converted dressing rooms, teletype instruments clattered. A special office backstage was walled with crammed file-cabinets, lighted by a low-hung bulb above a desk covered with secret communications. At this desk, tonight, an ebon-eyed man was working feverishly—the man who was commander-in-chief of the activities of the United States Intelligence the world over. He was known, even to his most trusted agents, only as Z-7.

His black eyes smoldered with a deep fire as he read the series of communications being brought to his desk—reports dispatched by his widely scattered secret agents.

... KT-NY... TANKER PACIFIC GIRL CARRYING CARGO OIL FROM CHINA TO STATES CANNOT BE REACHED BY WIRELESS... NOT ON HER COURSE... HAS APPARENTLY VANISHED... H-2,—SC....

The dispatch was from Shanghai, China. The next had been sent by wireless from an agent in Venezuela:

... KT-NY... FIRE ABOARD RIO BLANCA TANKER CARRYING OIL TO NEW ORLEANS... SHIP DOOMED CREW ABANDONING... SABO-TAGE CERTAIN BUT MEANS UNKNOWN... C-14 ABOARD....

The third bore the mark of the Intelligence sub-headquarters at Chicago:

… KT-NY… EXPLOSION IN SUPER-POWER REFINERY THIS CITY COMPLETELY DESTROYED PLANT…SABOTAGE ONLY POSSIBLE CONCLU-SION… ALL OTHER REFINERIES UNDER SPECIAL GUARD… ALIEN SUSPECTS CLOSELY WATCHED… SERIOUS OIL FAMINE IN CHICAGO… D-17, CI….

Z-7's fist slammed on the desk. "Sabotage on every hand! Every drop of oil as precious as gold and tons of it being wantonly destroyed!" He looked up as a dispatcher strode into his office, carrying a fresh communication. "Operator 5," he growled, "have you had word from him?"

"No, sir!"

The Washington chief groaned. "Fifteen hours since A-9's report! We've got to find Operator 5! Call every headquarters near the Texas fields and check at once. Find Operator 5 and Tim Donovan if—"

Z-7 SETTLED again to his chair, his face dark-lined as another dispatcher hurried out. His black eyes smoldered at the teletype which had come to his office the night previous from A-9:

… KT-NY THRU WDC-13… FOLLOWING PREVI-OUS INSTRUCTIONS RETURNED TO SUSPICIOUS WELL TO FIND IT IN FLAMES… NO SIGN OF OPER-ATOR 5 OR BOY… SEARCHING… A-9….

The message the dispatcher handed him read tersely:

… KT-NY… OIL PRODUCTION SMACKOVER

FIELD ARKANSAS DROPPING ALARMINGLY...
TWENTY WELLS CEASED OPERATION LAST
TWELVE HOURS... MORE ABANDONED EVERY
HOUR... SMACKOVER RESERVE EXHAUSTED...
LR-A....

Z-7 glared at a middle-aged man seated on the opposite side of his desk, R-9, working out of KT. "Another of our most valuable reserves is petering out! Inside this country and out, our supply is failing! A short year ago, oil from foreign countries was pouring into the United States duty free and we were protesting against it.* Now we're begging for oil at any price, and we can't get it! If this keeps up—"

Again Z-7 snapped to his feet as a wide-eyed dispatcher plunged into the room: "Chief! A message from Operator 5! He's on the air now!"

"Thank God!" Z-7 strode rapidly to the door. "Stay at my desk, R-9—wait for orders!" He walked quickly into the vast space behind the lowered curtain of the theatre, turned to a door standing open: "Hold Operator 5!"

---

* AUTHOR'S NOTE: A complicating factor in the oil situation inside the United States was the competition of foreign oil passing into the country duty free. While attempts were made to shut down American wells, to avoid over-production, floods of the black fluid from foreign shores flowed across our borders—from Russia, Venezuela and Roumania. This oil, produced by workers at wages far below the United States level, competed with American oil and undersold it. Lobbying in Washington by powerful oil factions had prevented the erection of a tariff barrier against this oil for the protection

"He's speaking now, Chief! Asking for you!"

Z-7 drew a chair to the table on which sensitive shortwave wireless equipment was placed. He affixed ear-'phones, brought a microphone close to his lips. Faintly he heard a voice speaking through a crackle of static—a far-away voice that brought a surge of relief to his heart.

"Put Z-7 on the air!" it was commanding. "Z-7 at once!"

"Z-7 talking!" the Washington chief exclaimed. "I've been trying to raise you for hours! Where are you?"

The distant voice answered: "First, Chief—have you had any word from Tim Donovan?"

"No—none!"

A BRIEF, tight silence followed. "Chief, I've been trying to locate Tim since last night, without results. I've waited to hear

of the American oil-worker. Senator Elmer Thomas of Oklahoma declared on this point:

"Who opposes this tariff on oil? The Standard Oil group opposes it. The Standard Oil group is the Rockefeller group. It is a $5,000,000,000 group!

"The Gulf Oil Company opposes this proposal. The Gulf Oil Company is reported to be the personal property of the Mellon family.

"The Dutch Shell group, a foreign corporation owned by the government of Great Britain, is here opposing this proposal. The Dutch Shell group is another billion dollar group. We are opposed by concentrated wealth in the gigantic sum of at least $7,000,000,000.

"The main opponent here is the Dutch Shell group, the greatest producer of oil in the world—527,000,000 barrels daily for the entire year!"

from him until the last possible minute before starting back East. If he sends a report, I'd like to have it at once!"

"Right! But for God's sake, where are you?"

"I'm aboard an army plane that has just left Brooks Field, Texas. I must reach New York as soon as possible. I have uncovered valuable information which must be checked while I'm on the way. Listen carefully, Chief!"

Operator 5's words lightninged through the night—through hundreds of miles of empty sky. Far across the country, slashing the air at top speed, a Martin bomber was carrying him. An ace service pilot was at the controls; in the observation cubby, hunched before the plane's short-wave equipment, Jimmy Christopher was speaking into a microphone.

His face was dark-lined, his eyes anxious. During a long, exhausting day, he had vainly sought word of Tim Donovan. He had recovered consciousness to find himself completely alone near the flaming oil-well; he had sought his way on foot to the nearest town. Every minute of the following hours he had devoted to intensive work on the case. Now, at the first free opportunity, he was flashing his report to his chief.

"I have here," he declared, "a revolver on which I have developed a set of fingerprints. I have classified them; they must be identified if possible. Note this, Chief! Section Three by One over One. Five over Seventeen. U over minus lower a. Parenthesis ten over upper M. Seven over six. Check at once!"

Z-7's pencil had darted the symbols on a sheet of paper. He ripped it off, thrust it into the hand of a waiting dispatcher, spoke again into the mike:

"Got it, Operator 5! Go ahead!"

"The man who made those prints operated the suspicious well near the *Oro Negro*, Chief. A-9's suspicion that some new weapon of war was being tested there is wrong. This man has somehow succeeded in pumping oil out of an exhausted well, and he has been storing it in another emptied reserve. He has disappeared; we must make every possible effort to locate him at once!"

"Stay on the air and we'll have the facts about him in a moment if his prints are on file."

"All right, Chief! That man was approached last night by Jaime Coronza. Coronza knows what the secret of that well is. He wants it—he is determined to get it. He also has disappeared, Chief, and we must find him, too. I am certain he is the center of a vast intrigue, trying to rob us of the last of our oil. Warn all our men who look for him that he is the most powerful and dangerous spy alive!"

"Coronza! You suspected that he was working in the United States! We'll use every means of finding him!"

"Our men are also to look for all signs of espionage conducted by the great oil powers—chiefly Great Britain, Japan and Russia. Coronza must be working for one of them—perhaps for all! It is certain that the most ghastly weapons are being used against us in this struggle for oil, and Coronza is using them!"

"Stand by!" Z-7 straightened as another shirt-sleeved man entered the room, carrying a card. "We have identified the fingerprints! That man is—*wait!*"

THE WASHINGTON chief peered in surprise at the card.

45

His black eyes smoldered with puzzlement as he spoke into the ether:

"He is Professor Norton Yerian, who has been affiliated with five colleges and universities in the East in the past twenty years. He has a New York address. It says here that he has conducted certain experiments in oil, but the nature of them is not given. The most important fact is that five years ago he was convicted by the Federal government on a charge of evading the income tax laws. He served three years as a prisoner at Atlanta!"

Jimmy Christopher's exclamation carried over the air. "One of his assistants was named Orth. Have you information on any of the others?"

"Yes! There is a man named Landis Fairhill, also of New York. At one time they conducted experiments in a loft on Murray Street, but have since abandoned the place. No new laboratory address is given."

"Chief," Operator 5 directed, "we must follow this lead as carefully as possible. Please get Diane Elliot at once, at Address

TIM DONOVAN

Y. Send her first to Yerian's home. She is to learn if possible where Yerian can be found. If that fails, she is to try to locate Fairhill. She can act as a newspaper reporter wanting their views on the national oil situation. If she fails to locate either of them, we must take a gambling chance!"

"Let me have your instructions!" Z-7 demanded.

"Insert in the *New York Times* personal column a cryptic notice addressed to Fairhill's initials, signed with Yerian's! Code the notice—message asking Fairhill to meet Yerian at one of our cover addresses. I'll take care of the further details when I arrive. Meet me, Chief, at Mitchell Field."

"Count on me to do both, Operator 5!"

"I'm convinced that Yerian possesses certain knowledge which is of inestimable value to the United States in this crisis. We've got to find that man! In the meantime, Chief—"

Z-7 broke in. "There are reports on my desk right now which prove beyond all doubt that the United States is the victim of a gigantic plot to cripple her through manipulating our oil supply. Within our borders, our wells are becoming exhausted—our remaining supply is being destroyed. Oil shipped to our shores from foreign ports is being kept from us by cunning, merciless sabotage. We have already been struck staggering blows. Thanks to you, we would only now be realizing our danger if you had not warned us long ago. Even so, our situation is desperate."

"I advise you to call for immediate reports about military activities from our agents in every important nation, Chief!"

Z-7 spoke sharply into the microphone. "Reports have already begun to come in, Operator 5. Japanese sea-spies are operating in increasing numbers on the Pacific. Alarming information is also coming to us from European capitals. By the time you arrive, I will have further information from our foreign agents. I will—"

"Chief!" A dispatcher, racing from the communications-room, touched Z-7's shoulder. "Teletype message, hot off the wire, mentioning Tim Donovan!"

Z-7 snatched for the yellow sheet "Stand by, Operator 5!" he snapped into the transmitter. "Word from Tim!" And he read the black words rapidly, repeating them into the microphone.

"The message comes from our headquarters in St. Louis, through WDC-13. It states that SLM received a telephone call from Tim Donovan a short time ago. The boy told them he had trailed a suspect on your orders—that this man was even then engaging a plane for New York. The plane took off at once and Tim followed by air. SLM checked at once and found that the boy is right on the job!

"Lord Chief, I'm glad to hear that!" A chuckle carried over the air. "I've always said that Tim is a better trailer that any man in the service! Order your men to watch all New York airports, and try to spot Coronza. The fact that he's—"

"Wait! A second dispatcher had hurried into the room, his face was pale. The hand that proffered the message to Z-7 trembled visibly. The Washington chief stared at the sheet and his eyes glowed darkly.

"The Crystal Refineries in East St. Louis have been destroyed by an explosion!" he exclaimed. "Word has just come in! Another valuable source of fuel eliminated! Good God, Operator 5, the oil spies in this country are making a concerted attack on us! We'll soon be absolutely helpless!"

"Coronza is directly behind that damnable piece of sabotage, Chief!" Operator 5's voice came back. "Find that man! I'm making top speed for New York!"

Z-7 backed from the microphone with his fists clenched and his jaw-muscles bunched hard....

CHAPTER 4
WAR CLOUDS GATHER

T HE SUN sent slanting rays across the great tarmac of Mitchell Field, Long Island, New York. At the barred gate, a sentry patrolled. Near it, two cars stood and the passengers who had come in them waited near the operations-building, peering into the sky. One was Z-7, his face pinched with anxiety. Beside him stood a girl, radiantly pretty, in her early twenties— Diane Elliot. Shading his eyes against the glare, his face wan and his blue eyes worried, was John Christopher, Operator 5's father, formerly Operator Q-6 in the United States Intelligence.

Far above, in the sunlight, wings flashed—a plane flying high. It banked into a descending spiral, sleek, powerful, its motor drumming. Diane Elliot watched with red lips parted, face glowing with eagerness. "It's Jimmy! I know it's Jimmy!"

She followed the sweep of the shining wings as the great Martin swooped lower. A year ago, Diane Elliot, a reporter for the far-flung Amalgamated News Service, had met Operator 5; since that time she had aided him valuably in numerous important cases. She was fearless and zestful in her pursuit of news; yet she respected the secrecy under which Operator 5's work must be done. Her face lighted happily as a helmeted head looked down from the observation pit of the bomber, and an arm waved.

"It *is* Jimmy!"

"Thank God he's back safely!" Z-7 exclaimed. "That boy is more valuable to his country at this moment than he has ever been before!"

"You can count on Jimmy completely, Chief," John Christopher declared quietly. "He'll come through."

Ex-Operator Q-6 had been forced from the service by a serious wound which constantly threatened his life. Two bullets, embedded so near his heart that no surgeon dared operate, forced inaction upon him. He felt high admiration for the achievements of his only son—unbounded pride that Operator 5 was carrying on his work with such signal success. His arm wagged an answer to a greeting from the pit of the Martin as it shuttled into a landfall.

Operator 5 sprang from the cubby as the trucks stopped rolling. Diane Elliot ran to him with skirt flying. She flung her arms around his neck; she pressed her full, warm lips to his. He backed away, laughing in confusion, his cheeks scarlet.

"Lord, Di! A greeting like that is certainly worth a non-stop trip from Texas!"

"Jimmy Christopher, you've only made about a hundred and fifty miles an hour. Next time," Diane admonished him, "come faster!"

Laughing, Operator 5 gripped Z-7's hand, and his father's. His smile faded as he asked quickly: "Any word from Tim?"

"None yet, Jimmy," John Christopher answered. "Great Scott, son, your eyebrows and eyelashes are burned off! What the devil—"

"The devil's work for sure, Dad," Jimmy Christopher answered quickly. "Di, have you followed the leads? Have you—?"

"Yerian and Fairhill are both missing. Jimmy," the girl told him breathlessly. "Their families don't know where they are. I've tried every possible way to locate them, but it's no good. It's impossible even to guess where they are."

"And Coronza?" Operator 5 demanded of Z-7.

"No sign of him!"

Jimmy Christopher's lips tightened. "I want your reports, Chief, as soon as possible."

"The Commander has turned his office over to us. This way!" Z-7 OPENED a door of the operations building and Jimmy Christopher strode into the room beyond. John Christopher closed the way tightly behind Diane. Pulling off helmet and gloves, Operator 5 settled at the desk and rapidly read reports which Z-7 placed before him. Each moment his eyes grew darker. At one wireless dispatch he peered intently:

> ... KT-NY... BY WIRELESS THROUGH WDC-13...
> S.S. EMPEROR OF PACIFIC REPORTS SHIP-FOR-
> MATION OFF NORTH HAWAIIAN GROUP... SHIPS
> DISTANT AND CAMOUFLAGED BUT COMMANDER
> NILES CONVINCED THEY ARE WAR VESSELS...
> NATIONALITY UNKNOWN... NO NATION REPORTS
> MANEUVERS AT THIS POINT BUT THEY ARE NOT
> U.S. SHIPS... REPORTED STEAMING FULL SPEED
> EASTWARD... POSSIBLE AIRPLANE CARRIER
> AMONG THEM... WAR DEPARTMENT ORDERS

MARCH OF THE FLAME MARAUDERS

VERIFICATION FROM PACIFIC NAVAL AIR-BASES.

Quietly Operator 5 declared: "Our own Pacific fleet is seriously hampered by an extremely limited oil supply, Chief. But months ago, the Japanese navy was assured by its government of a fully adequate reserve!" *

"Yes—that is true!" Z-7 exclaimed. "We are now surrounded

---

* AUTHOR'S NOTE: United States Ambassador Joseph Clark Drew, as well as the British and Dutch ambassadors, were startled into a vigorous protest: against a drastic action of the Japanese Foreign Office last November in respect to foreign oil companies operating in Japan and Manchukuo.

The National Oil Business Law proclaimed by Emperor Hirohito contained amazing provisions. It required all foreign oil companies doing business in Japan to build additional storage tanks and to keep always on hand a six months' supply of petroleum in addition to their normal needs; and the Japanese government reserved the right "in case of necessity" to purchase all petroleum at its own price, which might be below cost or purely nominal—that is, the government might, if it chose, confiscate all such oil supplies. In effect, this provided that a huge oil reserve for the Japanese navy must be accumulated and maintained by potentially enemy countries at their own expense—unless they wished to stop doing business in Japan!

In Manchukuo, Japan proceeded to set up an absolute oil monopoly, banishing all foreign oil from sale until the entire output of the Japanese-owned refineries was sold.

This proclamation and monopoly, according to a dispatch of the Associated Press on Oct. 24, is part of the Japanese navy's plans to dominate the economic development of Manchuria and control the empire's oil supplies from the standpoint of national defense.

by nations which have guaranteed themselves of a far greater fuel supply than ours. But—exactly what do you mean?"

"Chief," Operator 5 came alertly to his feet. "I have expected this development. I have been waiting for it to come. I am positive that an attack is going to strike us very soon—while we are crippled by lack of oil for our battleships and air forces—when we will be unable to repulse it!"

"An attack? By what nation?" Z-7 demanded.

Operator 5's eyes narrowed. "I need charge no single nation with the attempt, Chief. Until we are able to identify the camouflaged battleships, which are at this moment steaming toward our Pacific coast, I will not say. But we know full well that for long months, Japan has been strengthening her naval and military forces—strengthening them largely with raw material brought from the United States!"*

"The Japanese war budget is larger for this year than it has ever been before!"

"We also know," Operator 5 continued, "that similar prepa-

---

*AUTHOR'S NOTE: As 1934 drew to a close, the war machinery of the world began to move with greater speed. In the Orient, activities became feverish, complicated by the Japanese attitude toward the coming naval-ratio congress with the United States and Great Britain.

Japanese papers began waging a propaganda campaign for war against the Soviet In the *Charbin Shimbun* appeared this statement: "Nine-tenths of the Japanese population in Manchuria want war. All possible sacrifices must be made in preparation; for example, even three-year-old children, when they are playing war games, should learn how to handle a gun and

rations have been going on all over the world. We have not been blind to it. But we have not realized that the whole military

saber, and it must be impressed upon them that war is enjoyable, and that we must love war."

Shortly afterward, the Japanese Ministry of Finance approved a Navy budget for 1935 of 490,000,000 yen ($137,000,000) and an Army budget of 450,000,000 yen ($126,000,000).

On November 20, at Yokosuka, Japan's new 8,000-ton cruiser *Suzuya* was launched in the presence of Emperor Hirohito, and simultaneously at Kure the keel of a 10,000-ton aircraft carrier was laid—the first of two such vessels to be built at a cost of $12,000,000 each. The *Suzuya* is the third of the new type of warship built by Japan—ships which, despite their classification as "light," are one of the most heavily armed fighting ships afloat, excepting only capital ships.

In the new Japanese budget was also an item of 160,000 yen for the development of a Tokyo-South Seas air line—the first step in establishing swift air-connections between Japan's Pacific islands and mandates. Japan was actively discouraging foreigners from her mandated islands. She refused two requests for United States naval vessels to cruise through them.

Late in the year, Japan was buying 61 per cent of all the scrap iron exported from the United States. A sharp increase showed in exports of scrap to all nations, while Japan's amount exceeded all the rest of the other nations combined. The metal, said a United Service dispatch dated November 13, was being used largely for the manufacture of shrapnel. In addition, seventeen decommissioned United States destroyers were being converted into raw materials for Japanese munitions, according to the *Philadelphia Inquirer:* these ships had been sold by the United States navy to a Brooklyn concern,

strength of the world might be turned against us—while we are rendered helpless through the exhaustion of our oil supplies! We have unknowingly made ourselves the prey of any nation which chooses to attack us—and attack us, I assure you, they will!"

"This thing you suspect—?"

"Means the end of the United States unless we find the power—the oil power—that is necessary to protect us. The world has been waiting for our wells to become exhausted. Hostile nations have bided their time while we have squandered our oleic wealth. They have been waiting for the day that must come soon—the day when a conqueror will be able to flood his military forces across our shores with no fear of opposition."

"God! It's not possible!"

"IT'S NOT only possible, Chief—it's inevitable!" Jimmy Christopher faced Z-7 squarely. "You know only too well what the complete failure of our oil supply will do to us. It will cripple our battle fleets—make them float helpless, without power, in the water. It will make it impossible for our airplanes to get into the air. It will make troop movement slow, if not altogether impossible. It will deprive us of our tanks, separate our

which scrapped them, and the charge was made that two steamers a week were carrying the scrap into the Orient, presumably to Japan.

At the same time, newspaper correspondents cabled reports that an alliance was in the making between Germany and Japan to offset the startling announcement of an alliance between Russia and France. Moscow officials declared they had documentary proof of the new alliance.

These facts, correlated here for the first time, present an astounding picture.

armies when they move from our sources of munitions and ration supply. There is one thing in the world a military machine absolutely needs—oil! Without it, we might as well have no army, no navy, no air corps at all!

"Behind this sabotage which is striking at us, Chief, there is a purpose. Our few remaining producing wells are being destroyed for a definite reason. Shipments of oil sent to the United States, from American foreign reserves, are disappearing or going up in smoke for that same reason. We are watching the working of a gigantic plan—and the purpose behind that plan is to cripple the United States!"

Z-7 stared, his face turning white, into Operator's 5 dark eyes.

"Isn't it enough," Jimmy Christopher demanded, "to know that many of the battles of the World War were fought for the possession of oil-fields? Isn't it enough to know that France once faced certain defeat by Germany because her fuel supplies threatened to fail?* We are facing exactly that situation now,

---

* AUTHOR'S NOTE: Oil played a vital part in the first World War—so vital that, had not the United States rushed to the rescue at one stage of the conflict and supplied her with desperately needed oil, France would have suffered immediate defeat. This amazing statement is based on a communication from Georges Clemenceau, then Premier of France, to President Wilson, in December, 1917, one of the blackest periods for the Allied forces. Clemenceau declared:

"A failure in the supply of petrol would cause the immediate paralysis of our armies and might compel us to a peace unfavorable to the Allies. Now the minimum stock of petrol computed for the French armies by their

Chief—and the most appalling part of it is in my opinion that

Commander-in-Chief must be 44,000 tons and the monthly consumption is 35,000 tons. This indispensable stock has fallen today to 28,000 tons, and threatens to fall almost to nothing if immediate and exceptional measures are not undertaken and carried out by the United States. These measures must be taken without a day's delay for the common safety of the Allies, the essential condition being that President Wilson shall obtain permanently from American oil companies tank steamers with a supplementary tonnage of 100,000 tons.... The safety of the Allies is in the balance. If the Allies do not wish to lose the war, then, at the moment of the great German offensive, they must not let France lack the petrol which is as necessary as blood in the battles of tomorrow."

General Foch at this point was insisting that France did not possess enough oil to last more than three days in the event of another heavy German drive. The United States supplied the heeded oil.

Germany was also battling for oil supplies. Ludendorff, in his memoirs, states: "As Austria could not supply us with sufficient oil, and as all our efforts to increase the production were unavailing, Roumanian oil was of decisive importance to us." Field Marshall von Mackensen thereupon led an attack into Roumania, and plundered the properties of British, Dutch, French and Roumanian oil companies. Baku, on the Eastern front, was also a center of strenuous struggles over oil-fields. Oil was the dominating factor in the Near East and Balkan campaigns.

During the height of the struggle on the Western front, the consumption of oil was 12,000 barrels a day.

When Germany found its oil supplies cut off, when the Allies retook the Roumanian fields, Germany was defeated. Lord Curzon, commenting on

there is no way out of the danger!"

Z-7 echoed in a gasp: "No way out? You mean that we can do nothing to save ourselves?"

"If hostile nations concentrate their forces against us from both the East and the West, they will be able to bottle us up. They can establish an embargo to every port in the United States. They can make it impossible for us to receive a single drop of oil from any receive abroad. They can force us to rely wholly on the stores within our boundaries—and those supplies are almost gone.

"From the wells of the United States at this moment there is not enough oil flowing to supply our normal needs. Hour by hour, our reserves are diminishing. That fact is a natural phenomenon. As far as our knowledge goes now, complete exhaustion is as inevitable as the whirling of the earth and the flowing of the tides. No man possesses the power to create new oil within the shell of the earth. There is only one hope—one remote hope that we must gamble on—"

"In God's name, what is that?"

"The million to one chance that—"

Operator 5 broke off, listening. In the air above Mitchell Field, a faint vibration pulsed. The wind carried it in a throbbing gust as Jimmy Christopher strode out of the office. He peered at a plane circling overhead, driving downward. As Z-7 came to

the outcome, declared: "The Allies were carried to victory on a flood of oil," but he might have added, to complete the truth, "on a flood of American oil."

his side he asked quietly: "You arranged for that personal notice to be printed in the *Times*, Chief?"

"Yes. They have the copy now. The papers will be on the street with it late this evening."

"That, too, is a chance," Jimmy Christopher observed as he continued to watch the plane winging down. "I'm banking on Fairhill's not having heard from Yerian—not knowing where Yerian is. Yerian may not be near New York, but Fairhill probably is. Somewhere in the millions of New York—*it's Tim!*"

JIMMY CHRISTOPHER had seen a head peer down from the circling plane—a head covered with a cap pulled low against the whipping of the wind. He signaled jubilantly, and the passenger of the plane wagged back at him. Operator 5's dark eyes gleamed.

"If Tim has learned where Coronza went, Chief, it's a highly valuable lead. If he hasn't—?" Jimmy Christopher's lips pressed hard. "Not knowing what nation Coronza is working for is a terrific handicap. He may be serving any one of half a dozen European countries. He must be identified with one that has been preparing desperately for war*—but now it's impossible

* AUTHOR'S NOTE: In Europe, the machinery of war also began to accelerate with the waning of 1934.

France was warned late in November that Germany was building a mighty military machine and could, by this year, throw 5,500,000 men into action within a few days. Leon Archimbaud, Reporter of the Budget for France, estimated that Germany had also between 3,500 and 4,000 trained pilots and a large number of airplanes in reserve; he added that the Krupp factories

to guess which. Tim!" Operator 5 shouted the name as he began
to run across the field. "Tim, old-timer!"

were turning out heavy cannon, artillery, field guns and powerful mortars in
large numbers. Marshal Franchet D'Esperey declared that "The situation
seems at feast as grave as in 1914."

The world was startled, also in late November, by the offer of Soviet Russia
to back France with her powerful army in the event of war with Germany.
Russia's army then numbered 800,000 with reserves of 15,000,000 and
France's standing army numbered 600,000 with reserves of 6,000,000—
therefore France would have an alliance of almost 20,000,000 men in the
event of war.

General Victor Denain, Minister of Air of France, at the same time asked
the Chamber Air Committee for 3,500,000,000 francs (about $230,000,000)
to modernize the French air fleet so as to outstrip Germany's—while, on
December 15, France's defaulted war debt to the United States reached the
figure of $160,000,000.

The 1935 naval budget of France is 2,903,000,000 francs and it provided
that work be speeded on the construction of "pocket battleships" similar
to Germany's. At the same time, a new battleship, the *Strasbourg*, was laid
down at St. Nazaire. France's submarine *Minerve* was launched in October,
to be followed early in 1935 by the large under-water vessel the *Ouessant*.

At Vitry-le-Francois, a "rehearsal of war mobilization" occurred, calling
15,000 reservists into action for four days. The French police began a "puri-
fication" of Paris, raiding bars, cafés and dance halls, searching for weapons
and demanding identifications. This ostensible search for spies resulted in
438 arrests on suspicion in three nights.

On all sides, indications of approaching war were plain to he seen.

The plane weaved down. Its trucks touched and a storm of sand whipped back from the prop. Before the crate ceased rolling, Tim Donovan leaped over the cowling and raced toward Jimmy Christopher. The Irish lad greeted Operator 5 joyfully.

"Jimmy! Gee I'm glad to see you! I told the pilot to head here on a hunch, Jimmy! I knew you always used this field! I didn't know what had happened to you and—"

"Good work, Tim! I want your report on Coronza right now!"

The boy's eyes were wide and glistening with happiness at his seeing Jimmy Christopher again; but immediately they clouded. Suddenly he blurted:

"I—I lost him, Jimmy!"

"Lost him, Tim? He shook you? How?"

Operator 5's grave eyes studied the boy's face. "I—I guess I'm no good, Jimmy," Tim faltered. "I tried to stick on his trail—but he spotted me following him. We ran into a storm over Illinois—a bad thunderstorm. He flew right into it. I did my best, Jimmy—but when we got out of the storm, he was gone! I'm sorry!"

Operator 5 straightened, his lips pinched. "Okay, old-timer. You can't be blamed for that. If it had been at all possible to stick to him, you'd have done it." His arm tightened across the tough lad's shoulders as he turned to Z-7. "Chief, Coronza has probably already reached New York in some way. Check our men!"

Z-7 hurried again into the office. Operator 5 followed him slowly, thoughtfully, as Diane Elliot and John Christopher hurried to greet Tim. At the telephone the Washington chief's voice rang: "KT! Z-7 calling! Contact all men watching the

62

airports and get reports on Coronza. Connect with the most important fields now. I'll hold the line!"

Jimmy Christopher turned quickly to the Irish lad. "Tim—you're worn out, but I need your help. I've got a detail that you can handle better than any man in the service. It's another job of trailing, and one of our regular operators might be spotted. If our play fails, it can't be repeated—we'll be up against a blank wall. It's got to come through; we've got to locate a Professor Yerian. That's why I want you to handle it, old-timer."

"Sure, Jimmy!" the boy exclaimed. "You can count on me for anything!"

"Di, you'll help too? I need both of you."

"Jimmy Christopher, you know I'll do anything you ask of me!"

"Good girl! Di, you're to be in the classified-ad section of the *Times* Building tonight at the moment the first copies of the next issue come off the presses. You're to spot any man calling for a letter addressed to a certain code number. When you spot him, Di, telephone Tim. Z-7 will tell you what the code-number is—where Tim can be reached.

"Old-timer, you'll be on watch. The message that man picks up at the *Times* Building will take him to a certain address, and you'll be watching that place. He'll come out again, and you're to follow him no matter where he goes, no matter how far. It will be dangerous, Tim, but that man must be kept in sight in spite of everything!

"Once he reaches a second meeting-place, you're to telephone

LANDIS FAIRHILL

JAIME CORONZA

me immediately at Address X—and wait. It's one of the most important jobs you ever tackled, Tim!"

An exclamation burst from Z-7's lips. He turned to peer darkly at Operator 5. "KT has checked up the chief airports around New York, and the report is—nothing! No sign of Coronza! It means he slipped past our men. It's certain that he's already in New York. Wait!"

The Washington chief listened intently as the receiver rattled, as a voice carried over the wire from secret headquarters KT. A keener light was shining in his eyes when he turned away from the telephone and faced Operator 5 squarely.

NORTON YERIAN

OKATO HINZU

"The oil situation," he declared, "has forced the government to drastic action. The President has just issued a proclamation for the rationing of our remaining oil supplies. He has appointed a Federal Oil Commissioner in an attempt to assure our defenses of as large a supply of oil as possible. Now the whole country will know the real danger we're facing! It means terror!"

Jimmy Christopher's eyes grew dark. "The President," he said, "has taken a very necessary action, but—that alone cannot save us. It will delay the complete exhaustion of our oil supplies, but it cannot prevent it. We still face the same terrible danger."

"Yes—I know! But what can we do? In God's name, what can we do?"

"I repeat, Chief," Jimmy Christopher said in a tone so low it was almost a whisper, "there is only one possibility of saving ourselves. Only one thing now that will keep the nations of the world from attacking the United States like wolves leaping upon a helpless animal. It's a million-to-one chance—a hope so remote—"

His voice faded. His eyes grew midnight dark. His fingers strayed unconsciously to the little golden charm on his watch-chain which symbolized the end of all things....

CHAPTER 5
MIDNIGHT DANGER

OVER THE length and breadth of the United States, a strange stillness settled—a hush of fear, warning of a paralysis creeping upon a great nation....

The streets of the greatest cities in the country became weirdly quiet. Where once swift traffic had flowed, only a few cars moved about. Automobiles were being left in their garages their tanks dry or containing only a small reserve of the fuel that had suddenly become precious. Those that moved along the thoroughfares excited as much wonder as the first which had appeared in the days of the "horseless carriage." Drivers were stopped by mounted police and questioned; rumors flew that cars were being confiscated, their fuel tanks drained and the gasoline turned over to the government.

Giant interurban busses stopped operating. Trucks abandoned deliveries. Airplanes ceased soaring from the airports of the chief municipalities; sky traffic became non-existent. Thousands of gas stations stood dark, their underground tanks empty, their pumps locked. A few which retained a small supply posted exorbitant prices. Taxi services in the great cities ceased to exist. Great transoceanic passenger liners stood in their docks around New York, Long Beach, San Francisco and all other ports, their sailings canceled. The blood of modern life was ceasing to flow—oil!

Paralysis!

In streets where no gasoline motors whirred, newsboys screamed the headlines of extra editions flooding from the presses:

"No Oil Sold Without Permit After Noon Tomorrow!
"Fuel Supplies Confiscated for Army and Navy!
"No Fuel Received in U.S. Past Twenty-Four Hours!

"Country Terrorized by Preparations for War in Europe!"

OVER A coast-to-coast network of broadcasting stations, announcers repeated the startling Presidential Proclamation and added their interpretations:

"This drastic measure is being more rigidly enforced than the restrictions on gold when the United States abandoned the gold standard. The proclamation provides for heavy fines and imprisonment for the hoarding or misuse of fuel supplies. It calls upon all persons or firms which hold fuel supplies to surrender them to the government, with drastic penalties for violation. In brief, oil and fuel have become more precious to the United States than gold!"

Over the bleak roads leading from the few remaining oil-fields of the United States which could produce petroleum, weighty tank-trucks crawled. In their reservoirs sloshed barrels of the black stuff that had suddenly become inestimably valuable. On the trucks, armed infantrymen rode. Ahead of them and behind them, other trucks traveled, carrying armed guards in the uniform of the United States army. From the dwindling reserves of the country, every possible drop of black power was being taken, for the use of the nation's defenses.

In a score of cities, oil refineries were posted with heavy guards. To them still other protected tank-trucks came; from them streamed the crystal fluids for which the motors of a nation were starving. The United States government was policing every valuable drop of liquid fuel.

In the greatest city of the nation an electrical tension tightened. New York's streets were weirdly quiet. No headlamps gleamed; no motors whirred; no taxies moved; no passenger buses were operating. Millions, who had never given a thought to the subject of the smelly, black stuff that flowed from the earth hundreds of miles from the metropolis, now spoke of it in awed tones, in voices that paid reverence due to vital liquid power.

At the Crossroads of the world—Times Square, New York—thousands thronged the streets where traffic had ceased to move. They raised fear filled eyes to the ribbon of words sparkling around the *Times* Building. On the flashing board, news-dispatches were unwinding, tightening the tension in the air.

U.S. STRIVING—TO MAINTAIN—DEFENSES—FUEL RUSHING—TO ALL—FRONTS—SEVERE CRITICISM—IN CONGRESS—ON SLOW WORK—BEGUN LAST YEAR—FEVERISH—PREPARATIONS AGAINST—POSSIBLE ATTACK—

Inside the classified-ad section of the *Times* Building, on the ground floor, Diane Elliot peered out upon the anxious crowds. She stood at a desk, filling out a blank form with meaningless words, tearing it up, writing another. For an hour, since being warned by Operator 5 through KT that the first copies of the *Times* were leaving the presses, she had covertly watched the desk. In one pigeon-hole of the rack behind it, coded H-251, a single letter waited. Again and again, the girl's eyes glanced at it—each time a man or woman approached the desk.

She tightened when she observed a thin, serious-faced man peering into the triangular office through the glass swinging-doors at the rear. He backed away, stood aside, waiting until several persons at the desk left. When the office was empty, except for Diane Elliot, he entered quickly. He spoke in a low tone to the clerk behind the desk; and the clerk's voice carried to Diane.

"The gentleman who left this letter requested identification of anyone coming to claim it."

The lean man hesitated, then withdrew his wallet. He displayed a driving-license to the clerk. Promptly the clerk handed him the letter. Without opening it, he thrust it into his inner pocket and strode out.

DIANE STEPPED quickly to the desk. She knew that the clerk behind it was Operator G-11 of the U.S. Intelligence. She proffered a blank, heard G-11 say quietly: "J. Fairhill!"

Diane Elliot answered quickly: "I see I've made a mistake. I'll rewrite it." And carrying the blank form, she turned away. Casually she returned to the desk, watching the man who had identified himself as Fairhill standing beyond the glass doors. He had opened the letter and was reading it. The girl knew the words typewritten on the page:

LF—623 East 50th, first floor right, at once. Extremely urgent. NY.

The lean man hurried out the entrance, into the thronged streets where no car was moving. She hastened down a flight of steps and slipped into a telephone booth. She called a number quickly.

In a room on the first floor of a sooty rooming-house, far on the East Side of Manhattan, on Fiftieth Street, a bell shrilled.

Tim Donovan grasped up the telephone. He had been waiting for hours in a room dark and silent, used as a "cover address" for the receipt of confidential communications by the United States Intelligence. He spoke quickly into the transmitter and Diane Elliot's voice carried over the line:

"Fairhill's just claimed the letter, Tim! I'm calling KT right away. On your toes, old-timer! We've found him! Jimmy's long gamble is winning. Follow it through!"

"I won't let him out of my sight!" the boy exclaimed.

He broke the connection, turned to a table, and made sure that a sealed envelope was lying on it. He snapped on the table light so that the brightest shine fell on it. He hurried out the door and along the windy street. When he paused, he was in the shadow of a wharf-house at the edge of the East River. The murky water lapped beyond, unlighted by the beacons of any boat, for all oil-burning craft were now tied up at their docks—useless.

Anxiously Tim Donovan waited. Each passing minute strained his nerves. He shrank back as two men sauntered along the street, crossing toward the rooming-house opposite. One of them was speaking grimly:

"It's been comin' and now we're caught in it! I know what fightin' over oil means, I tell you! I was in Mexico when the revolutions started. All that blasted trouble was over oil—big corporations fightin' each other for concessions. Huerta, Villa—all of 'em were black with oil. The United States sent Pershing down with troops, didn't we? All on account of oil! The damn' black stuff is poison—and we're starvin' for it!"

"The British've got plenty," the other returned. "The Russians and the Japs've got plenty. Every nation on the face of the earth has got all they need—except us! God, we're in for it!"

The first snorted. "This is only the beginnin'. Look at 'em fightin' down in South America—Paraguay and Bolivia. That's been a war for oil.* The United States has got to do somethin', I tell you! If we can't get oil in any other way, we've got to fight for it!"

Tim Donovan watched the two men saunter into the rooming-house and climb the stairs. He realized that the terror lying behind their words was echoed in the heart of every United

---

* AUTHOR'S NOTE: The war of the Gran Chaco, between Bolivia and Paraguay in South America, which has been raging for more than two years, is a battle for tin—and oil. Munitions-makers have fostered the conflict—and oil has paid for the armaments. There are vast oil reserves in Bolivia, but no coal, and no way of getting the oil out of the country. It cannot be piped up the Andes; therefore Bolivia's need is for a port on the Paraguay River, which would open her way to the entire world—a way now closed by Paraguay. Victory by Bolivia would mean a rapid development into a modern industrial state. And victory by Bolivia would mean the end of Great Britain's domination of the tin field—tin that is precious in the making of armaments, a product of which England holds a virtual world monopoly. In the spring of 1934, Great Britain proposed to the world an embargo of munitions to the two combatants in the Gran Chaco—apparently a commendable move toward peace. It was not realized until later that this move came at a moment when Bolivia was back to the wall, when an embargo would have made her defeat and Paraguay's victory certain! Here again great powers may be seen struggling for oil supremacy.

States citizen. The urgency of his mission tightened him to greater alertness. He watched the shadows along the street, and glimpsed a slow movement in the gloom.

A LEAN, tall man was walking toward the rooming-house. He paused near it, glancing about warily. When he pushed through the door, he turned to the room on the right—the room which Tim Donovan had left. The boy saw him knock, hesitate, then enter. Across the drawn blinds, a shadow moved—and Tim knew that the letter on the table had attracted Fairhill's attention.

He knew its message:

> LF—Cannot remain here longer. Afraid I am being watched. Only safe place is the lab. Go there at once. I will be waiting. NY.

Tim Donovan crouched low in the shadows as the lean figure of Landis Fairhill again appeared in the light of the door. The lean man strode in the direction he had come. The boy hurried across the street, his short legs swinging swiftly to match Fairhill's quick strides. The tall man turned quickly and began striding north along a weirdly quiet street.

The boy trailed his quarry expertly, dodging Fairhill's backward glances, hurrying to round corners. Each time the lean man passed out of view Tim raced to sight him again. Block after block the trail lengthened, until Fairhill again turned east. Tim followed him into the gloom flanking the East River, toward a squat building perched on the very edge of the brackish water.

In front of it, Fairhill paused, glancing around warily. The sign on the door beside him bore a notice reading: CITY

TRUCKING CO. Fairhill opened it with a key, passed inside. Tim Donovan darted close, heard footfalls ascending a flight of stairs. He noted, through the sooted windows, that the rooms on the lower floor of the building were deserted; he backed away, watching the panes above, but no light appeared. Yet he was certain that Fairhill had entered rooms above.

The door did not yield when he attempted to open it. He turned away anxiously. On the far corner, he saw a gasoline service station, the beacons of its empty tanks unlighted, its house dark. Behind the pit, a car was sitting. The boy hurried through the shadows, slipped to the dark side of the car, and lifted the front-seat cushion. He groped and his fingers met cold metal. He turned away with eyes shining, gripping a tire iron.

He returned cautiously to the window of the structure which Landis Fairhill had entered. He worked the sharp edge of the tool beneath the sash of the window and pried. The boy's face twisted with a strenuous effort. A dull snap sounded; the sash jerked up. Quickly the boy raised it, legged over the sill.

He crept through a musty room, opened a door. A hallway lay beyond; a flight of stairs led upward. Tim Donovan stole to the steps, testing each before he placed his weight on it. His breath came in short pants when he reached the top and peered at a closed door. A spot of light was shining through a large keyhole beneath a big metal knob. Tim Donovan brought his eye to it.

He peered across a brightly-lighted room; he saw a wall which appeared to be metal. On it, pressure-gauges were affixed, and beneath the gauges stood black drums and compressor-tanks. Footfalls echoed within the room; the lean figure of Landis

Fairhill came into the boy's line of sight He backed away with eyes shining triumphantly.

He had found the secret laboratory of Professor Norton Yerian.

Every muscle tight, he crept down the stairs. His mind was humming with a remembrance of Operator 5's urgent orders. "If you spot the laboratory, 'phone me at Address X at once. It's the most important job you ever tackled!" Breathlessly the boy crept to the window he had opened. He thrust his legs through, he ducked out, and—*attack!*

SWIFT POWER struck at Tim Donovan with a vicious slashing sound. A savage blow jarred his head with blinding force. He threw up one arm instinctively, to protect himself, as dark forms rushed at him. His mind whirled as he tried wildly to scramble free, but a sharp-nailed hand clamped around his throat. A fist smashed cruelly into his face. Tim Donovan slumped against the wall, feeling his arms and legs gripped, while he strove desperately to retain consciousness.

"Take him in! Quick!"

Tim Donovan heard the order faintly, the words accented and sibilant. He felt himself lifted through the window. He was forced to the floor and a tight strand whipped around his wrists. He struggled grimly to escape the powerful hands that pinioned him. Tears streamed from his eyes—tears of fury as he realized the hopelessness of the fight. He was twisted over while a hard hand clapped his mouth. Suddenly he was jerked up.

"Take him up with us! Careful!"

Two men lifted Tim Donovan off the floor as the third turned to the dark stairs. Wide-eyed, his vision bleared, he saw that the leader held an automatic. Facing the door, the square-shouldered men knocked. The thumps reverberated hollowly within the room beyond. Footsteps approached the door; through it a tense voice asked;

"Who is that?"

"Open! Quick!"

The square-shouldered man tensed as a bolt slid back. A line of light appeared; an eye peered out. Instantly the man with the automatic thrust inward. He slammed the door wide, whirled to cover Fairhill with his weapon. The light gleamed bright in his icy eyes.

"Get back! Back, señor!" Through the door he commanded to his men: "Bring the boy in!"

The two men jerked Tim Donovan into the room. He stared, blinking with pain, at the pale man backed to a wall which consisted of metal plates riveted together. Within that steel box of a room, Fairhill stood cowed before the gun in the hand of the tall, swarthy man. He thrust the metal door shut, shot its bolt into the socket.

"Stand where you are, and in a moment we shall talk business, no?"

The Spaniard's gesture signaled the two men holding Tim Donovan across the room. They pushed open a connecting door in the wall of steel. Beyond lay a second room, the light of a bare bulb shining from the black walls upon compressor tanks and drums and strange devices. Toward a chair standing beside a desk in one corner, the two men carried Tim Donovan. They thrust him into it. One of them whipped another length of wire from his pocket and bound the boy to it tightly.

They whirled away to the other room. "Watch him closely!" came the guttural voice of the swarthy man. *"Por Dios,* he will talk or he will die!" Footfalls rang on the metallic floor, and the Spaniard stepped into the rear room to peer at Tim Donovan. His thick lips curled into a leering smile.

"More than one can follow the same trail, *amigo mío!"* he exclaimed. "I am grateful that you have led me to this place! We have been long searching for it. Here I shall learn a secret which you will never know!"

He strode to the desk. Tim Donovan's gaze followed his every move as he searched the drawers. For a long time, the Spaniard persisted, peering at closely tabulated pages, flinging them aside, probing further until at last the desk was emptied. He stepped back with his swarthy face suffused with angry color. He strode to the door and snapped:

"Search! Search everywhere!"

He leveled his automatic as he strode through the door. The two men shouldered in past them. Tim Donovan noted now, as his vision cleared, that one was saffron-skinned and slant-eyed; the face of the other was greasy, his eyes a glinting black. They ignored the boy as they began to search again through the scattered papers.

The Spaniard's voice carried from the next room. "You know where the data is hidden, *amigo mío,* no? You will save yourself great anguish, perhaps, if you tell us the place now."

Fairhill blurted: "I don't know! I don't know!"

"We shall see!"

Tim Donovan strained to free his hands from the wires biting through his skin, but the effort resulted only in excruciating pain. As the two men abandoned their search and trod into the forward room, his aching eyes shifted to the desk. His face flashed pale with the thought that leaped into his mind when he saw a telephone sitting far back, on the rear edge of the blotter. He knew it was impossible to reach, impossible to free himself… but….

"Now!" The Spaniard's voice was a threatening whisper. "We will induce you to decide to talk, Señor!"

A stifled gasp came from the next room. Tim Donovan scarcely heard it; he was peering at the telephone, his mind racing. In the course of their search, the men had moved the desk-blotter so that one corner protruded beyond the edge of the desk. Tim strained forward, endeavoring to bring his head close to it. If he could catch the corner of the blotter in his teeth, if he could drag the telephone forward, if he could spill it into his lap and whisper a few words…!

A sudden, sharp scream rang from the forward room. It was vibrant with pain and terror. It wailed off, and the throaty chuckle of the Spaniard followed.

"Don't do that!" Fairhill's breathy plea came. "Oh God, don't!"

"I shall be obliged to persuade you, *amigo mío,*" the swarthy man answered, "until you give me the information I wish."

Tim Donovan stared again at the telephone. Precious seconds were ticking by—minutes punctuated by strangling cries and choking protests from Fairhill in the next room—

and those minutes were Tim Donovan's only opportunity. He bent forward, bearing against his bonds, straining with all his strength.

If he could bring the telephone forward, if he could drag it off the desk and speak a few words—a few quick words…!

CHAPTER 6
THE FLAMING DEATH

A YOUNG man wearing a trim Chesterfield and a black Homburg jauntily tilted approached the staid apartment house, in the East Sixties of Manhattan, on foot—on foot because Fifth Avenue, ordinarily humming with traffic, was empty, and no taxi was available. The doorman greeted him, as he passed inside, with: "Good evening, Mr. Walsh!"

"Good evening," Jimmy Christopher answered.

An elevator carried him to the eleventh floor; a key of which no duplicate existed admitted him through a door of steel veneered to look like mahogany. In a tastefully furnished bedroom Operator 5 paused to peer at the headlines of the newspapers he had brought.

MYSTERY CRAFT OFF EAST COAST!
Submarine, Believed to be New Type Airplane
Carrier, Seen Lurking Near Coastwise Lanes!

Operator 5's darkened eyes shifted to another glaring headline:

OVERSEAS AIR ATTACK ON UNITED STATES DECLARED A POSSIBILITY!

Jimmy Christopher's lips twirked grimly as he dropped the papers. He swung toward the window a strange contrivance which sat upon an anchored table. He released a ratchet, unwound forty feet of rope ladder from a drum, lowering it over the sill. He pushed outward a flexible neck, the end of which carried a box that seemed to be a camera with a protruding lens. With easy confidence, he swung out into the darkness.

He descended into the space of a passageway that lay far below; at the end of the ladder he swung, caught the railing of a balcony on the adjacent apartment-house. He climbed over, removed his electric torch from his pocket, and shot its beam upward. The gleam actuated a photo-electric cell, a relay, and a motor. Uncannily, the rope ladder coiled upward and the window above slid shut.

Operator 5 passed through a dark apartment, into a hallway, paused at a door and pushed a silver button inscribed: *Carleton Victor.*

Carleton Victor, the whole world knew, was a photographic portraitist to whose Fifth Avenue studio the great of the world flocked. His crystal lens snapped renowned dignitaries, industrial leaders, social celebrities; each sitter was flattered by the favor of his attention. The name of Carleton Victor signed to a photo-portrait was in itself a credential of importance. He was admittedly a peerless artist with the camera.

Operator 5's touch upon the button brought a cool-faced

manservant to the door, one who bowed respectfully and greeted him with "Good evening, Mr. Victor."

Not even the estimable Crowe, gentleman's gentleman extraordinary, knew that the identity of Carleton Victor was a convenient cover for the secret activities of America's Secret Service ace. Operator 5's smile faded as he entered and paused.

"What on earth, Crowe," he inquired, "is the matter? Are you ill?"

Crowe bowed wretchedly. He was wearing thick gloves. Around his neck a heavy woolen muffler was wrapped. His pointed nose was an unbecoming red and he was visibly quaking.

"No, sir," he said. "At least, sir, not yet, but I am afraid I'll catch my death. You may notice, sir, that the apartment is miserably cold."

"It is." Carleton Victor's breath was frosty as he spoke. "It is beastly cold. Have you spoken to the superintendent, Crowe?"

"Yes, sir. His answer was scarcely satisfactory, sir. It was something about oil. It seems that the furnaces are oil-burning, sir. Why that should make any difference when we need heat, I cannot understand."

"You can't?" Carleton Victor looked startled. "Is it possible, Crowe, that you are persisting in your incredible habit of neglecting to read the newspapers?"

CROWE SUPPRESSED a sneeze. "I never read the newspapers, sir," he answered with dignity. "I consider them unimportant, sir, if I may say so. I shall speak to the superintendent again, at once. I shall absolutely insist upon our having a comfortable degree of heat."

"By all means, do so, Crowe." Carleton Victor smiled as he opened a closet. "He will probably try to put you off with some weak excuse, but you should insist. If he says something about there being no oil whatever available in the United States, simply ignore it, Crowe." Victor stepped into the closet and closed it.

"Quite right, sir," Crowe addressed the door.

The closet was sound-proofed; it contained nothing but a telephone. Once inside it, Carleton Victor ceased to exist; Operator 5 reappeared. He lifted the receiver and called a secret number. The voice that answered said:

"Oriental Hotel."

"Room 2020, please."

"There is no Room 2020 in this hotel."

"In that case give me 2025."

Signals exchanged, Jimmy Christopher tipped a cam set into the wall; it threw into the line a frequency-distorter which made eavesdropping impossible. The voice of Z-7, speaking at headquarters KT, came over the wire immediately.

"Chief! Have you had word from Tim?"

"None!" Z-7 answered. "Diane Elliot reported, as you know, but that was two hours ago. Either Tim's trail has led him far afield, or something has happened to him. Immediately word comes, I'll relay it to you. Until then—is there nothing we can do but wait?"

Grimly Operator 5 answered: "Nothing but wait, Chief—if you are sure our men are on the job at the producing wells and at our reserves abroad. Have we still not received any shipments of oil from South America?"

"Not a drop! I have reports here stating that two more oil-tankers have apparently vanished, while on their way to this country. A third has caught fire. Two wells in the Spindle-top field in Texas have somehow become ignited and tons of precious oil are burning at this moment. Our situation is rapidly becoming more desperate!"

"You have instructed our men to look especially for the Scheele detonators? It's certain, Chief, that those deadly devices are being used against us again.* The fact that they are time-fuses means that our watch must be absolutely thorough—for by the time any fire breaks out, the sabotage agent is certain to be far from the scene."

"There are no reports of Scheele fuses being found. They are being used with an uncanny shrewdness. We are doing our best!"

"Your search for foreign espionage agents, Chief—?"

"We have definitely established the fact that there are, in this country now, secret agents from every oil power in the world. Our operators abroad have sent reports which make this

---

* AUTHOR's NOTE: The incendiary fuses mentioned here by Operator 5 were used for sabotage work in the United States by German secret agents during the first World War. They were the invention of a German chemist, Dr. Scheele, and were first used by Captain Franz Rintelen von Kleist, who was sent secretly to the United States by the German War Office with the chief purpose of destroying shipments of ammunition from America to the Allies. The detonators, secretly placed among the cargo by Kleist's men, were the cause of the sinking of many ammunition transports. They still constitute a dangerous weapon in the hands of skilled *saboteurs.*

certain. Some of these men must be engaged in sabotage; yet I cannot believe that Great Britain, especially, would stoop to such damnable work. There must be another excellent reason why those spies have stolen into this country."

"There is, Chief! Depend on that! They are seeking the most precious prize in the world. Until we hear from Tim—until we are able to find Professor Yerian, or Fairhill—I cannot say more. But if I'm right, Chief, there is no treasure in the world to equal the value of the thing those spies are after."

"I don't understand."

"Wait, Chief, until I am sure of what I believe. I can only say now that it is the one hope the United States has of escape from complete and utter disaster."

"As you wish, but—if there is any hope at all, we must play it to the limit. Even if we are able to supply our defenses with sufficient oil, for a time, the fact remains that industry now lies in a state of paralysis. This is not only because oil is needed as fuel, but because oil is the basis of manufacture of so many products in daily use—of so many Industrial chemicals. Every branch of our daily life is being thrown into a state of catalepsy by our lack of oil!" *

"I know, Chief," Operator 5 answered gravely. "A long

---

* AUTHOR'S NOTE: Crude oil is not only the source of gasoline, naphtha, kerosene and lubricating oils, but it enters into the daily life of every person in hundreds of ways. Four hundred articles in common use are derived from oil. We eat oil products, drink them, wear them. The by-products would make a long list, including candy, sugar, varnish, paint, leather, rubber, asphalt,

chance—and we can do nothing but wait! Ring me at once, when word comes from Tim and—"

"Wait!" Z-7's voice snapped. "There is a message from the communications room. Let's listen! I'll cut you in!"

A CLICK sounded as Operator 5's nerves tensed. Over the line came, suddenly, a shrill scream—a cry of agony, of exhaustion. A far-away voice spoke gutturally. Fire sparkled in Operator 5's eyes as he heard it. And then, sibilantly, another voice spoke in a whisper—faint words that Jimmy Christopher strained his ears to hear.

"Tell Operator 5! Tim Donovan reporting! Address—" There the voice broke off, and Jimmy Christopher listened with caught breath while, from beyond, another wail of agony sounded. Then, quickly, Tim Donovan mentioned a number and a street. "Second floor! Fairhill's here! They're torturing him! The room's steel—steel!"

A sudden clatter followed, as though the distant telephone had dropped to the floor. Tim Donovan did not speak again.

"Chief!" Operator 5's voice crackled. "Send one of the service cars for me at once! Detail three of our best men to go with us! Hurry it! One of those voices I heard was Coronza's!"

"We're starting now!"

"Wait!" Jimmy Christopher's mind raced. "If they're beyond reach in that room! Chief, bring with you several cans of Special Item 45! Get that, Chief—45! It's highly important!"

alcohol and medicinal agents. The list of industrial chemicals derived from petroleum is so long that it fills a volume of 1,200 pages.

The line clicked off. Tensely, Operator 5 thrust open the door of the soundproofed closet; out of it stepped Carleton Victor. He saw Crowe just entering from the hall and signaled quickly for his hat and coat. The manservant, as he helped Victor into the Chesterfield, declared coldly:

"The superintendent is most stubborn, sir. He declared he had no oil. 'Very well, then,' I said, 'order some at once!' He had no answer for that, sir."

"I fancy not!" Carleton Victor turned quickly to the door, drawing on his Homburg. His blue eyes shone darkly. "Crowe, while you are here, in this miserable cold, you may picture these same conditions multiplied a million times from coast to coast. You are feeling only a suggestion of the untold hardship and suffering that is sweeping the country. You know nothing yet of the terrors that will certainly follow. Nations tearing at each other's throats, Crowe—over the slimy remains of a dead world!" *

Crowe's eyes widened. "I—I beg your pardon, sir?" he gasped. But the door had closed; Operator 5 was striding grimly away....

ALONG FIRST AVENUE, an automobile sped—the only car in motion on that broad thoroughfare. It raced northward past intersections without slowing, for there was no cross-

---

* Author's Note: The theory of the formation of oil below the crust of the earth is that hydrogen and carbon from the remains of preexisting plant and animal life, chiefly microscopic marine and swamp life, were combined under high pressure and heat. Thus Operator 5 states an exact truth when he says that petroleum is the remains of a prehistoric world.

town traffic to fear and the signal lights, still flashing, were a mockery. It swerved east; it drew sharply to the curb. From it, five men alighted—men who hurried toward the river through the deepest shadows.

Operator 5, an impeccably clothed figure completely out of keeping with the dismal neighborhood, led the way; Z-7 followed him closely; behind them strode three trusted agents of the United States Intelligence. They paused to peer at a moldering brick structure across the street. They noted the number on its door, that one of its windows was standing open.

"Tim telephoned from that place. Watch yourselves!" Jimmy Christopher warned. "J-9, cover that door. F-3, take one side of the building. Guard the other, W-4. If the men inside that building attempt to escape, stop them at all costs. One of them may be carrying the most valuable document in the world! To your places!"

Operator 5 brought his automatic into his hand as the three undercover agents drifted across the street. Their movements were silent; they blended away in the gloom. Jimmy Christopher waited tensely before he said: "We're going in, Chief. Guard the stairs. Now—give me the tins of 45."

Z-7 removed two flat metal cans from his pockets. Operator 5 slipped them into his coat. With quick, sure strides he crossed the street. He paused, listened at the window; he slipped through. Z-7 followed him into the musty room. They crept up the stairs, slowly, listening. It was not until they reached the head of the flight that a sound from beyond reached their ears.

It was a scream of pain. It was followed by words spoken in

a hysterical rush. "I'll tell you! I'll tell! There—that drum—in a can inside it! Oh, God, stop!"

A guttural voice followed: "Look first!"

Footfalls rang on the metallic floor beyond the door which Operator 5 now faced. He whispered urgently: "Ready, Chief!" and twirled his gun in his hand. He brought its butt forcibly against the wood and the blows echoed. Instantly all sounds of movement inside ceased.

Jimmy Christopher leaped the instant the aperture appeared, gun leveled on the men!

Sharply Operator 5 commanded: "Open the door, gentlemen!"

A breathless silence followed, until a sibilant voice spoke: "Wait! Get back! They can't get in here! The door, the walls, the ceiling, the floor—everything is steel! Let them try to reach us!"

A second voice exclaimed: "It's here! I've got it! It was hidden all the time in the drum of oil! A sealed can sunk—"

"Quiet! *Por Dios!* Wait—and watch your chance!"

Then again, tight silence.

Operator 5's signal drew Z-7 toward him. He threw his shoulder forcibly against the door. The dry wood crackled. Z-7 joined Jimmy Christopher's second attack and a panel splintered. Again and again they flung themselves with all their strength. Backing away, Jimmy Christopher ripped a panel loose and exposed a gleaming black slab beyond.

"They're right—that door is steel!" he exclaimed grimly. "We can't possibly break it down. It's bolted, Chief." He drew Z-7 aside and spoke in a whisper that could not carry into the room.

"We're stalemated. But this must not develop into a dangerous game of waiting. There's no time to get an acetylene torch. Remember, Tim's in there—if we give them the chance they may use him as a hostage. We've got to force them out—now!"

"How?"

"Coronza has found something in there—probably the thing we want—the thing the United States must have to survive! Take no chances on letting them slip away, Chief, once they're out. They're coming through that door—I promise you!"

Z-7'S DARK eyes followed Operator 5 anxiously as he

hurried to the rear window. He pried the sash open, leaned out and peered upward. Quickly he climbed on the sill and came erect. Balancing himself precariously, he reached upward to the rusty gutter on the edge of the roof. Flattening his hands beyond it, he raised himself with a strength-draining effort.

He kicked, sent glass spattering inward from the window, and braced his feet on the frame. A second pull burned his muscles with the effort of raising his waist to the level of the roof. He kicked upward, rolled, and snapped to his feet. Quietly he trod to a spot which, he calculated, was directly over the center of the room in which Coronza was enclosed.

Quickly he drew the two cans of Special Item 45 from his pockets. He pried off the lids, stooped, and trickled black powder from the containers in four lines to form a square three feet across. The dust was an improved thermite. From the cans he removed also several strips of silvery ribbon—magnesium. He inserted them into the black powder, struck a match, and ignited their upper ends.

The magnesium burned with a blinding white flame, sending white fumes upward, forming a white ash. From the strips, the flame crept into the black powder, creating an even more intense heat. Quickly, the square became a pattern of blistering flame—fire so hot that the toughest metal must liquefy under it. Operator 5 stepped back quickly, the glare shining in his face, watching the lines of white hotness sink through the roof while streamers of flame shot upward.

Through the timbers the thermite ate its way swiftly—to the black steel slab below. Immediately, the metal glowed red, then white; streams of sparkling steel flowed molten. At the edge of the deepening chasm, Operator 5 stood poised, gun ready, the light beating through his closed lids, the terrific heat blasting in his face. He heard a shout from below—a sudden clanging crash.

In the roof, a square section had dropped away—an open rectangle had appeared through the steel ceiling of the room below. The vicious sizzling of the thermite carried upward through the opening along with the dismayed shouts of the men in the room. Jimmy Christopher leaped the instant the aperture appeared. He dropped through the flaming hole, twisting in midair, his gun glittering level with the swiftly moving men even as he dropped.

Swift shots rang from the automatic in Jaime Coronza's hand. Deafening echoes clashed as the revolvers of the other two espionage agents joined the attack. Operator 5 returned the fire grimly as slugs spattered on the steel walls, rocking the room with a confusion of sound. He whipped toward Coronza as the yellow-skinned agent darted to the door.

A swift shot of Coronza's smashed the brilliant bulb burning in the ceiling. Glass fragments flew as darkness flooded the room. Operator 5 darted aside, his gun weaving, as red fire splashed out of the gloom. A square of light appeared as the door was flung open and a swiftly moving form became silhouetted against the wall beyond.

"Stop them, Chief!"

Out of the darkness, a heavy form leaped, throwing staggering weight on Operator 5. He wrenched away, driving out a stiff-armed blow, glimpsing the faint glitter of a slashing gun in the dark. Quick steps sounded behind him; a gun blasted again.

The voice of Z-7 rose in a warning shout to the men stationed outside the building. A flare of fire sprang through the doorway, into the twisted face of Operator 5's attacker, even as a gun swiped savagely toward his head.

Operator 5 drove stiff fingers to the neck of the man striking the blow. As with an uncanny magical power, the swarthy assailant's movements froze instantly. Paralysis seized him; he spun under his own momentum and toppled. Jimmy Christopher darted toward the door to see a blot of flame on the opposite hallway wall, to see Z-7 firing swiftly down the stairs.

Operator 5 sprang through, his automatic spitting. At the base of the stairs, the yellow-faced man was poised with one raised arm swinging forward. From his long-nailed fingers, a gleaming glass sphere flew. Operator 5 leaped aside as the Oriental whirled away and Z-7 shouted. Past his head, the glinting ball whizzed to strike the wall behind him and burst with a roar.

Flame spattered from the point of impact. The concussion of the fire-bomb spilled Operator 5 sideward. He went down the stairs with two long bounds; he ducked out the window as two sharp shots cracked. Glass spattered above Operator 5's head from a dark form hurrying along the street. And the darkness was flickering with red light—a shine that drew Jimmy Christopher's eyes in horror.

AT THE corner of the building, a man was staggering—a man enveloped in snarling fire! One of the secret Intelligence agents had been struck by a firebomb hurled by the escaping spy. Its explosion had drenched him with searing flame. A scream of

93

torture tore from his throat as he broke into an insane run—a stumbling, crazy race toward the water lapping below the edge of the dead-end street.

Grimly Operator 5 whirled past the building. Fresh flames were gusting upward—from the Intelligence car! It was enveloped in a cloud of snarling crimson. Another fire-bomb had hurtled doom upon it. Jimmy Christopher, gun leveled, sprang past it as the *whirr* of a motor sounded beyond. He saw a sedan dart past the intersection, saw light flash in the swarthy face of the man at the wheel. Jaime Coronza snapped two quick shots at Operator 5—and whisked from sight!

Jimmy Christopher spun back in breathless dismay. Jaime Coronza had slipped into a car powered with illicit fuel; it was carrying him away swiftly while the Intelligence sedan crackled in flame. Operator 5 raced back toward the brick building.

At the edge of the water, a moving fire was gleaming—a human torch. The undercover agent struck by the flame-bomb leaped into the river—into eternity—just as Jimmy Christopher caught a glimpse of him. A second operator was slumped against the building, moaning, wounded, leveling a gun at a crouched yellow-faced figure. Operator 5 recognized the slant-eyed face: "Hiroto Yenzi!"

The escaping espionage agents had tried to fight their way clear with murderous savagery, but only Coronza had escaped. Jimmy Christopher sprang up the stairs to see Z-7 playing the stream of a fire-extinguisher on the blazing hallway wall. His torch lighted the way as he sprang through the dark, steel room, into the lighted one beyond. In the chair, beside the desk, in the corner, Tim Donovan was striving desperately to tear from his bonds.

"Easy, old-timer!"

Operator 5 swung the boy's chair aside and snatched up the telephone which Tim had kicked beneath the desk. He rattled the hook rapidly. When a girl's voice answered, he snapped: "Police headquarters, quick!" Immediately the connection went through he exclaimed: "Operator 5 of the United States Intelligence talking! Signal all squad cars to search for a sedan being driven by a Spaniard! Capture him if possible! Has your radio fleet gasoline?"

"A little! The call's going out now!"

Jimmy Christopher turned away grimly. "Coronza will slip them—he's clever enough for that!" he exclaimed. He twisted quickly at the wires binding Tim Donovan to the chair. "Good work, Tim!"

The boy wrenched away from the loosened wires breathlessly. "Jimmy! Are you all right?"

"Never touched me, Tim!"

Operator 5 sprang back into the forward room, his torch cutting through the smoke. He played its beam on the swarthy face of the man whom he had felled with a jiu-jitsu blow. He exclaimed: "Pietro Ferro!" The flash-ray swung to a chair in the corner—to the slumped figure of Landis Fairhill.

Fairhill had also been bound; he had fallen forward in a faint. His collar was torn open; his throat was swollen and lacerated; around his neck still dangled a loop of wire which had been used to torture him. Jimmy Christopher snapped at Tim: "Phone for an ambulance!" and quickly examined Fairhill. He found a faint, irregular pulse and his lids lowered grimly.

Z-7 strode brusquely into the room. "We've got to get Landis to a hospital at once, Chief!" Operator 5 declared. "He's got a bad heart—he may not survive this. Coronza forced him to talk and—"

Turning, he brought the shaft of his light upon a drum of oil near the wall. A circular cover had been pried loose; drippings of amber disclosed that something had been removed from it. Operator 5 straightened as Tim Donovan's voice, speaking into the telephone, carried breathlessly from the next room, as Z-7 stepped closer.

"We've got two dangerous international spies, Chief—Ferro and Yenzi—but Coronza carried something away with him. He succeeded in getting—" Operator 5 broke off. "Help me with Fairhill, Chief! That man must be revived—he's got to tell us what Coronza stole. If it's Professor Yerian's process, the United States is doomed!"

CHAPTER 7
BLOOD OF THE WORLD

B ACK AND forth across the white hospital room, Operator 5 paced. He and Z-7 and Tim Donovan had accompanied the ambulance which had rushed Landis Fairhill to the hospital. In the adjoining room, Fairhill was now being treated by a physician. They had waited with burning impatience for almost an hour for word about Fairhill's condition. Jimmy

Christopher listened intently as the quiet of the corridor was disturbed.

He peered out the door to see a stretcher being wheeled into the room opposite Fairhill's—evidently a new patient being admitted. He forced himself to relax while Z-7 telephoned headquarters KT. Tim Donovan painfully rubbed his bruised wrists and watched Jimmy Christopher. Still no signal came from Fairhill's room; the agony of waiting whitened Operator 5's face.

Z-7 turned from the telephone grimly. "We have only seen the beginning of this situation," he began levelly. "Lack of oil is hampering the police in their protection of our cities. There is a wave of rioting and crime all over the country. Even worse than that, this crisis is giving a dangerous opportunity to every radical group in the country. There are thousands within our shores rising against us. We cannot learn yet what power is behind them, but it is breeding serious trouble.

"Besides that—!" Z-7 paused, moaned. "More news of oil refineries being destroyed! Ships carrying oil to our shores disappearing! We have just received word of two tankers that are adrift at sea, helpless, their rudders destroyed. Our enemies are seeing to it that we will be completely helpless!"

"More work of *saboteurs!*" Operator 5 snapped. "Chief, this means that whatever we do, we must act rapidly. Time is precious. While we still retain a small oil supply, there is some hope that we may survive, but once it is gone, not even Professor Yerian's secret can save us. Once we are without oil, once our enemies strike, we will be lost even if we learn—"

Jimmy Christopher broke off as a step sounded, twisted to the door. It was opened by a grave-faced man in a starched jacket who had a stethoscope hooked around his neck. He was Dr. John Wharton, the heart specialist who had been called to attend Landis Fairhill. Operator 5 demanded quickly: "Is Fairhill able to talk now?"

Dr. Wharton's head wagged. "His condition is very serious. He is suffering from *angina pectoris*, and the shock almost killed him. You may talk to him, provided you are careful not to overtax him. His life hangs in the balance."

Operator 5 smiled tightly. "His life—and the existence of the United States! Doctor, please stand by. That man must live to tell us what we must know!"

He strode to the door of Fairhill's room, with Z-7 and Tim Donovan following. They entered quietly. Beneath spotless sheets, Landis Fairhill was lying, face wan, eyes unnaturally bright. His beseeching gaze clung to Operator 5's face. Jimmy Christopher regarded him intently and drew a chair close. He spoke quietly:

"Mr. Fairhill, the men who tortured you are enemies of the United States. Two of them have been taken into custody. I am a servant of our government. I want you to help in this very real crisis. Help is absolutely necessary!"

Fairhill's eyes widened. "I know what you want! You want to learn—"

"Several things—all highly important," Jimmy Christopher interrupted. "First, where is Professor Yerian?"

"I don't know! I thought I was going to meet him tonight, but—! I don't know where he is!"

JIMMY CHRISTOPHER peered into Fairhill's face. "I am sure," he said soothingly, "that you do not know. But you do know that Professor Yerian has perfected a process which is beyond all doubt the most precious thing in the world today—a process of oil reclamation. You know also that the very existence of the United States depends upon using that process."

Fairhill's face grew dark-lined. "That is true, but—" He broke off, torn with an inner struggle. "Professor Yerian pledged me to secrecy!"

"He did not pledge you to help destroy your native country," Jimmy Christopher declared. "He did not make you promise to ally yourself with the most dangerous enemies this nation has ever known. No pledge you gave him can force you to throw your own family into the fires of war."

Fairhill stiffened. "I realize the danger of the oil famine. I do not wish to turn against my own country. But—"

"With a few words, Mr. Fairhill, you can bring strength back to the defenses of the United States. You cannot possibly keep the Yerian process secret, knowing that fact!"

Fairhill raised himself slightly, breathing quickly. "I—I can tell you a little. You must already know that the Yerian process is capable of bringing great stores of oil out of the earth—oil that is beyond reach by any other means."

"We know that," Jimmy Christopher conceded, "and so do our enemies. That is why you were tortured—that is why Professor Yerian is hiding from death."

"Yes!...." Operator 5 waited tensely while words trembled on Fairhill's lips. "The process is secret only in one important particular—but without that one detail it is almost useless. Listen carefully! Professor Yerian has achieved results far beyond those of any other experimenter—results incomparably greater than those of the universities trying to solve the same problem.

"He has surpassed the results obtained by the University of California laboratories, the California Institute of Technology, and both the Colorado and the United States Bureaus of Mines. He has made oil flow from wells which other experimenters have abandoned. It is possible, by the Yerian method, to get from twenty to one hundred times the original amount of oil from any well that has normally ceased to yield."

Jimmy Christopher asked cautiously, restraining his astonishment: "You are positive of that?"

"Positive! Every abandoned well in the country, if treated with the Yerian process, will produce again—twenty to one hundred times over the amount already taken from it. It means that the oil reserves of the country still hold enough crude to supply all the needs of the United States for a period of from fifty to two hundred and fifty years!"

Operator 5's eyes glowed darkly. Z-7 peered into Fairhill's face as though doubting the man's sanity. Yet Yerian's assistant was speaking with emphatic earnestness, with absolute conviction.

"You mean," the Washington chief asked quietly, "that if the Yerian process is applied to all our abandoned wells, the United

States will again be assured of all the oil she needs over a period of from one-half to two and a half centuries?'

"Exactly!" Fairhill elbowed up, his eyes gleaming. "We have repeatedly assured ourselves of that, both with laboratory apparatus and with work in the field. Listen! When a new oil-well is opened, the gas-pressure which forces the oil to the surface is sometimes enormous—sometimes higher than 2,500 pounds to the square inch. Under this pressure, as much as 1,000 cubic feet of gas are dissolved in a single barrel of oil. Once the gas-pressure drops, oil may still be obtained from the well, by pumping—but even so, an enormous amount remains in the earth, even after the well is abandoned."

FAIRHILL RACED on. "The oil still underground is held back by capillary attraction in the pores of the rock, by adhesion to the surface of the rock or sand, by friction in the minute pores. One cubic foot of sand may contain as much as 25,000 square feet of surface wet with oil—oil still imprisoned in the earth after the well has ceased to flow. The Yerian system draws this oil out of a well that has given up at first, say, 200,000 barrels of oil and then ceased yielding. Professor Yerian can make it produce from four million to twenty million barrels more. And this is true of every well in the world!"

Forcing his voice to remain low, Jimmy Christopher inquired: "How is that done, Mr. Fairhill?"

"By re-pressuring, by regulating the back-pressure, and with the use of a solvent gas developed by Professor Yerian. This gas is forced into the well until the pressure mounts to a certain point; it is then released and it carries oil up with it. The process is repeated until the oil once more ceases to flow. But, what I have told you is valueless unless you know the exact data discovered by Professor Yerian—unless you use the solvent gas he developed."

"That data?" Operator 5 inquired. "The formula for that gas? The means of producing it?"

Fairhill sank back to his pillow, breathing rapidly. "No one in the world knows the complete data—except Professor Yerian. No one knows the formula of the gas except him!"

"And, now," Jimmy Christopher asked carefully, "except the man who forced you to reveal the hiding-place of the outline for the process?"

Fairhill drew breath painfully into his lungs, summoning strength to speak again.

"Is that true?" Operator 5 demanded. "If it is, we must know it! If an enemy spy has come into possession of that data, we must also learn the complete details!"

"There is only one copy of the data," Fairhill gasped. "Only one copy and—"

"You surrendered it when you were tortured!" Operator 5 peered haggardly into the face of Z-7. The Washington chief's black eyes were smouldering grimly. "You gave up that information to an enemy nation while the United States is dying for want of oil!"

"No!" Fairhill jerked up again. "No! Professor Yerian has lived in constant fear that the secret of his process would be stolen from him. Day and night he has faced the danger of someone's robbing him of it. He has sworn to release it to no commercial pirates, nor to any imperial nation. He is a scientist—he studied the problem only as a challenge to his intelligence. Knowing that he was being watched—that his secret laboratory might be found, he—"

Fairhill was laboring for breath. Jimmy Christopher leaned forward tensely.

"He hid a sealed tube, containing data, in a drum of oil. *But that data is false!* It is not the true report! Anyone attempting to make use of it will get no results whatever! Professor Yerian wrote that false data only to mislead anyone who would attempt to steal his secret. Those papers—stolen tonight—are worthless!"

Operator 5 straightened with blazing eyes. "Thank God for that! Then where is the true data that—?"

"I did it only to save myself!" Fairhill blurted. "They were killing me—choking me to death! I had—"

"Where is the real data?" Operator 5 demanded again, his voice ringing. "Where is it hidden?"

Fairhill stared wide-eyed. "I don't know! No one but Professor Yerian knows! He has another laboratory somewhere—a place which he revealed not even to me. Perhaps it is there. But I could not tell you if I wished—not if the salvation of the United States depended completely upon it at this moment!"

Operator 5 peered in dismay. A burst of hot breath broke from the lungs of Z-7. Jimmy Christopher bent closer, his eyes shining imperatively:

"But the gas—the solvent gas! That is half the secret! The data could be found by laboratory experiment once the gas is brought into use. You know that formula?"

Fairhill started up again. "No! I do not know the formula for the solvent gas, either. I do know that, in manufacturing it, Professor Yerian has treated it electronically to defy chemical analysis. I know how to remove that electronic effect, so that it can be analyzed—and once it is analyzed it can be reproduced! I will tell you. Listen! Listen to every word. It is your only hope to—"

A SHOT blasted! The thunderous report of a gun jarred the room without warning. It crashed behind Operator 5 and Z-7; it wrenched a deep moan from the pain-wracked man on the bed. Jimmy Christopher sprang up instantly, even as a gash of red appeared across Fairhill's forehead, even as blood gushed from slashed skin and splintered bone. The power of the bullet flung Fairhill backward as Jimmy Christopher whirled.

He glimpsed a glint of gun-metal through a crack of the door—and a glittering eye. Instantly, the door snapped shut and fast footfalls beat over the corridor floor. From beyond came the startled cries of alarmed patients. Jimmy Christopher sprang to the door, snapping his automatic into his hand from its arm-pit holster. He leaped into the corridor to see a white-clad figure springing out of sight.

A bullet slammed at him when the man in the hospital garment darted past an angle in the hall. He darted aside as a gun thundered again, as another bullet screamed off the wall behind his head. Whirling into the L of the corridor, he glimpsed the white-clad man flinging a tubular object to the floor—a thing gushing white fumes. Jimmy Christopher leaped past it; and, hearing quick footfalls behind him, shouted back:

"Stay away, Chief! That's poison gas! Keep all doors dosed!"

He locked his breath in his lungs as he ran. In the center of the L corridor, the man in white was springing through the open gate of an elevator cab. The gun crashed again, and Jimmy Christopher saw the elevator attendant stagger against the far wall of the car, clutching his chest with hands that dripped red. Swiftly the panel began to slide shut; the car began to drop downward as the man in the hospital garment slammed the control switch.

Another bullet lightninged at Operator 5—and instantly his right hand became a thing of throbbing pain. The slug had spattered on his automatic, driving countless flecks of lead into his skin. His weapon dropped from his numbed fingers as he gave a flying leap toward the closing shaft door. The cab whisked out of sight below the floor level as Jimmy Christopher thrust his arm into the thinning open space of the panel.

A gasp of dismay broke from his lips when his automatic clattered over the sill and dropped into the shaft. Swiftly he thrust the sliding panel open. Far below the cab was gliding downward, past level after level. It would reach the foyer gate in a matter of seconds. Jimmy Christopher peered one instant at the black, steel cable to which the cab was suspended—a glistening, greasy strand flowing downward. He leaped…!

His arms and legs curled around the cable. He slid downward swiftly. The car was descending below him, but he allowed himself to slip at a much faster speed. Grease oozed through his fingers, gathered on his arms and legs, while he plummeted. As he neared the cab his muscles tightened to slow him. His feet touched the roof of the dropping car.

Gripping the cable with one blackened hand, he snatched at the catch of the leaf on the cab roof. It was an aperture through which workmen crawled to make repairs in the mechanism above the car; it opened easily. Below, in the cab, the man garbed in white was still hunched at the control switch. His glittering eyes turned upward as Operator 5 lifted the leaf—his gun lightninged.

Jimmy Christopher jerked back, and a slug screamed up through the opening, rattling high into the shaft. With his left hand he snatched at the buckle of his belt. His touch loosened it; he wrapped his fingers around the hilt of a thin-bladed rapier coiled in a narrow sheath of leather around his waist. He jerked it from its loops and it snapped straight; the sheath flew from it. He leaned forward. The gun in the hand of the man below leveled for another shot—and the lightning of his blade flashed downward.

Steel dashed steel. Operator 5 slashed the needle point across the fist gripping the gun. Red spurted and the man howled with wrath, fell back. Jimmy Christopher straightened, stepped into the square opening—and dropped. His soles smacked to the floor of the cab as he whirled, rapier glittering, his right hand swinging to the control switch.

The other man's red hand jabbed the gun toward Operator 5. Again the supple blade whipped to its barrel. Fire spurted; a slug rang against the metal wall of the cab. But so swiftly that his blade was visible only as a sparkle of light, Jimmy Christopher made the keen steel dance over the gun. Its magical power tore the weapon from the hand of the white-clad man. It thumped

106

to the floor of the cab as Operator 5 thrust the control switch to neutral.

A snarl of insane fury beat into Jimmy Christopher's face as the elevator bounded to a stop below the main floor level. His rapier whipped level and he warned: "Stay back!" In mad wrath, the other flung himself forward—full upon the glistening whip of steel. A tremor passed along the blade to Operator 5's hand. He peered into a face which suddenly blanched. He stepped back, lifting a blade that was now bright red. The man in the white garment clawed at the wall, gasping—slid to his knees, and rolled over....

OPERATOR 5 straightened grimly, peering at the square face, the staring blue eyes, the thatch of straw-colored hair. He thrust the control switch, started the car up. His lips pressed thin as floor after floor flicked past. When he brought the cab to a stop and opened the grille, he noted that the air of the corridor beyond was still misted in white. He ceased breathing, hurried to the door of Landis Fairhill's room.

He stepped through to find Z-7 stumbling from the bath, coughing painfully. The Washington chief slapped the door shut, pulled a window wide open and drew in a deep, gasping breath.

"I got that damned gas-fuse out of the hall!" he sputtered. "It's under water now—out! God—poison gas liberated in a hospital! That damned devil!" And the chief coughed again.

"He was Manfred Bethwig, Chief," Operator 5 declared grimly. "A German—another international spy, and almost as dangerous as Coronza." He peered at the still form on the bed.

"Keep getting fresh air into your lungs and the effects of the gas will pass. Tim—are you all right?"

"Sure, Jimmy!" the Irish lad blurted. "But that shot—it killed—!"

The boy broke off, staring wide-eyed. Jimmy Christopher nodded grimly; he drew the white sheet over Landis Fairhill's lax face, over the ugly wound in the forehead.

"Dead!" he declared quietly. "Killed at the moment he was going to tell us how we might discover the secret of the Yerian process ourselves. Killed so that the United States would keep starving for oil!"

He thrust out the door, crossed the foggy hallway. He warned several nurses, who were looking out, to keep back; without breathing, he strode to the windows and flung them open. Clean air gusted in as he returned to an open door—that of the room opposite Fairhill's. The bed was unoccupied. He returned to Fairhill's room and paused, his eyes shining dark.

"Bethwig was one of Coronza's men. He must have been watching the laboratory building—he saw Fairhill brought here by ambulance. He was clever enough to fake an illness and to get himself brought as a patient to the room opposite this one. Another bold move by that damnable espionage ring to keep us from getting that vital information!"

Z-7 mopped at his streaming eyes. "But we did learn that the Yerian process can save us from this oil famine. We did learn that there is some hope of escaping destruction!"

"It is the hope I'd already spoken of, Chief," Operator 5 declared, gazing bitterly at the bed on which Fairhill lay dead.

"If we can get the Yerian process, the oil famine will be ended. That is why Coronza and his men tried to get it—not only because it is priceless in itself, but in order to crush us—in order to keep from us the single item of knowledge that will save us! It proves again that Coronza's espionage ring is striving to make us the prey of foreign militarists!"

"Now," Z-7 declared, "there is only one way of our ever learning how to reclaim our exhausted oil-wells!"

"And that way," Operator 5 declared, "is a slim gamble, Chief. Telephone KT immediately, and direct a squad of our men to strip Yerian's laboratory. They are to take to our own analytical laboratories every drum, every tank, every device that Yerian used. They are to work night and day to analyze the gas in those drums—if possible, to learn the secret of the process.

"If they learn it," Jimmy Christopher continued quickly, "they are to begin work instantly with Yerian's devices—some of which are miniature models of oil-wells for testing purposes—in order to compile the data he has already obtained. This must be done—but I am afraid it is hopeless. I have a feeling that the gas will absolutely defy analysis, that getting correct data will mean years of experimentation both in the lab and in the field."

"The only answer, then, is to find Yerian?"

"To find Yerian—but not only that," Operator 5 warned. "He hates the United States. He intends to withhold his information. Finding him will not be as difficult as getting his data. That is a problem which no weapon—no force—can solve. But we must find Yerian, Chief—he *must* tell us the secret of his process. If we do not learn that secret—and quickly—the United States will soon cease to exist!"

CHAPTER 8
EAGLE PATROL

OPERATOR 5 closed behind him the door of the hospital room in which the spy Manfred Bethwig had hidden. From a closet, he removed the clothing Bethwig had worn before changing into the hospital garment. While Tim Donovan watched, he examined each article of clothing, searching particularly for hidden pockets. His blue eyes were filled with a deep, dark light as he straightened. Z-7 entered the room.

"Nothing, Chief," he declared. "Not a clue pointing to Coronza. Our trail has come to a dead end. Have you followed my suggestions?"

"Yes," the Washington chief exclaimed. "Six planes from Mitchell Field are taking-off now. Each pilot has orders to search this region thoroughly, to try to locate Professor Yerian's autogyro. It's a long chance, but they may hit upon a lead. Also, I have one of our best men listening in on the telephone-line of Yerian's home. Other men are watching his laboratory. We're doing everything possible."

Operator 5 nodded. "But we must find him, Chief! You may depend on it, Coronza is also doing his best to locate the professor. No word of him?"

"Police radio cars have not been able to locate Coronza or

his car—no. Evidently he slipped into some garage where he's covered completely. What more can we do?"

"Nothing more, Chief," Jimmy Christopher declared solemnly, "until we have a new lead!"

He stepped into a corridor now cleared of all traces of toxic gas. He said nothing until he left the elevator in the lobby with Z-7 and Tim Donovan. Striding out into the quiet street, where no automobile was moving, he said crisply:

"Phone me at Address Y, Chief, immediately if a break comes. We've got to be ready to act on the instant. Come along, old-timer!"

Tim Donovan trotted alongside Jimmy Christopher. Operator 5, absorbed in thought, did not speak during the quick walk to his father's home. He bought several fresh newspapers at the corner stand, opened the door of the house designated Address Y in the lexicon of the Intelligence. As he hurried up the stairs, Diane Elliot ran from the living-room to greet him.

"Jimmy—" the girl said anxiously, "if there's anything I can do to help—"

"There is, Di," Operator 5 answered. "Are you game to tackle an important job—and a dangerous one—right now?"

"Anything, Jimmy! Just tell me!"

Operator 5 warmly gripped his father's hand as he entered the living-room. He threw off his hat and coat. "You've already made sure that Professor Yerian's family don't know where he is, Di. His telephone is tapped and we've got men covering the house, but he may try to get in touch with his home by some way other than telephone, and he may know our men are watching.

I want you to go to his place. Tell the two men you're relieving them, and start watching that house. Stick on that job, Di, as you never have before!"

"Right!"

Diane hurriedly got into her coat, pulled a pert hat on her head, tossed a kiss to Operator 5, and ran down the stairs, powdering her nose. Smiling, Jimmy Christopher strode into the workshop located behind the living-room. It contained a chemist's bench, apparatus devoted to radio research, wood-working machinery and strange devices the nature of which were known only to him. He shut the door, and Tim Donovan, hearing him moving about, waited eagerly. When Jimmy Christopher came out again, the Irish lad lingered near.

"It's the stiffest case we've ever tackled, Dad," Operator 5 explained to Ex-Operator Q-6 as he took up the newspapers. "The United States is in the worst plight in its history. It's appalling to think that its whole future depends on the knowledge of a single man—Professor Yerian—and his process for revivifying our oil reserves."

"On two men, son," John Christopher declared quietly. "On Yerian and you!"

OPERATOR 5 smiled slowly. "All I, or any other man can do," he insisted, "won't help a particle without that process. We've got to learn the secret. If we don't, we are utterly lost. And the military machines of the world are waiting for the moment when we will lie helpless before an attack. Look at that!" Jimmy Christopher indicated a black headline on the newspapers he was holding:

MYSTERY SUB AGAIN SIGHTED! HOSTILE
CRAFT LURKING IN GULF!

Strange Underwater Vessel, Nationality Unknown,
Disappears When Seen. South Coast Feels Rising Terror.

"Our Coast Guard is searching for that sub, Dad, but they are hampered by shortage of fuel. Terror—yes! It will grow. That sub means a planned invasion—there is no disguising the fact. Before this, the world battle for oil has meant revolutions and invasions and attacks. Now, unless we stop it, the United States is going to be trampled out of existence!"

Operator 5 sank wearily into a chair. Tim Donovan perched on the arm of it, his eyes now clouding with disappointment. Jimmy Christopher looked at him and smiled.

"Something wrong, Tim?"

"Gee, I thought maybe you'd be showing me a new trick, Jimmy," the lad said plaintively. "I bet you haven't got any more than can fool me as the others did."

"We'll see about that, Tim!" Operator 5 rose alertly. "Keep your eyes open, because I *am* going to fool you. I'll give you a demonstration of a magical production of fire and water right under your eyes. Now watch!"

Jimmy Christopher opened a drawer of a chest, removed a black cloth from it. He tossed it to Tim, and the boy examined it minutely. Finding nothing suspicious about it, he returned it, and Operator 5 flapped it in the air.

"Nothing concealed in it, Tim—nothing whatever. Yet, when I spread it over my arms, like this—when I make a mystic pass, like this—and when I invoke the magical powers—there!"

Jimmy Christopher whipped the cloth away and disclosed in his right hand an ordinary drinking-glass filled to the brim with water! Tim Donovan's eyes opened wide. Operator 5 passed the glass to him carefully, to avoid spilling it.

"Any guesses, Tim?" he asked with a smile. "You see, the glass is so full that a slight move makes the water run over the brim. I couldn't have had that tucked in my pocket somewhere, could I?" He tossed the cloth aside. "As for the second half of the trick, I'll do it right before your eyes! Watch!"

He opened his coat with his right hand, reached into his inner pocket with his left and produced, before the astounded Tim, a candle—burning!

"There you are," he remarked, placing the lighted candle in a holder. "Got it figured out?"

"Gee, you couldn't have kept a burning candle hidden in your pocket either, Jimmy!" the boy exclaimed. "You've certainly got me fooled again! How'd you do it?"

"Take a few minutes to figure it out, old-timer!" Operator 5 settled again into the chair, and his smile faded. He found his father gazing at him seriously. Ex-Operator Q-6 asked quietly:

"Jimmy—need we depend on our oil wells, or even on Yerian's process? Aren't there other ways of producing oil?"

"Yes—but they are beyond our reach, or else the means have never been developed to a scale big enough to supply our needs, Dad," Operator 5 answered. "The Bergius process,* for instance,

---

* AUTHOR'S NOTE: In 1910, after years of patient experimenting, Dr. Frederick Bergius, at Heidelberg, developed a process of producing oil from coal.

produces some oil, but the patents are controlled by foreign trusts. The government has already started a move to use our shale deposits, but it will take time to develop—too much time. In all the world, Dad, Yerian's process is the only one that can possibly rescue us. And—"

"Jimmy—I'm stumped!" Tim Donovan interrupted. "Come on, tell me how you did it!"

OPERATOR 5 chuckled as he rose again. "Simplest thing in the world, Tim. Bring me that cloth. Thanks!" Out of its folds, Jimmy Christopher removed a device of rubber. "You see, Tim, it's nothing more than a rubber cap that fits over the top of the glass and keeps the water in. I prepared myself for the trick

Since Germany is without petroleum resources of her own, the German chemical trust, I.G. Farbenindustrie assumed the patents. Ten million barrels of gasoline leave the I.G.F. factories of the Leunawerke every month. The great Imperial Chemical Industries, Ltd., of England, has also acquired the German patents and is constructing a huge plant in Billingham, to cost 2,500,000 pounds and produce 100,000 tons of oil annually. The entire output of this plant will be reserved for the Royal Air Force. The Trust which controls the Bergius patents allows them to be used in Europe for military purposes, but not for the production of oil for commercial purposes. Many secret agents have tried to discover the secret of the ingenious system, but without success. It is, for example, impossible to take photographs of the process equipment, for all the important parts of the factories are provided with hidden ultra-violet ray machines, working constantly, which render any film or plate brought near them entirely useless! Germany is therefore assured of a protected supply of fuel for her engines of war.

when I went into the workroom because I expected you would ask to see one.

"I simply filled the glass with water, fitted the cap on, and put it in my hip pocket A few waves of the cloth and I slipped the glass from my pocket, so you couldn't see the move, and pulled the cap off. I left the cap in the cloth when I tossed the cloth away. In the same way, magicians produce fish-bowls, with real fish swimming in the water, though in that case the bowl comes from a *servante*—a secret shelf concealed behind a chair or table. Easy, isn't it?"

"Sure!" the boy exclaimed. "But the candle isn't that simple, Jimmy!"

"Almost, Tim. Watch." Operator 5 blew the candle out and tugged at the charred wick. It came away in his fingers. He removed a small box from his pocket, and drew something that looked like a match from the box. He showed Tim that it was a special Lucifer—a string heavily waxed, instead of a stick, with combustible material on its end. One of these he fitted into the candle so that it looked like a wick except for its tip.

"You can buy these at any magical supply house, old-timer. It's a special kind of wax match that strikes with scarcely a sound. Look here. Inside my coat, just about the inside pocket, I have a small square of black emery cloth sewn. The candle, prepared as you see it, was in my inner pocket—unlighted, of course. As I removed it, I rubbed the head of the wax match against the square of abrasive—and the candle appeared before your eyes lighted! You stand in such a way and hold your coat so that your audience cannot see the candle until it is burning."

"Dog-gone!" Tim exclaimed. "I thought you couldn't fool me, but you certainly did, Jimmy—and easily, too!"

Operator 5 allowed the boy to try the candle trick; and Tim eagerly began practicing the use of the rubber cap on the glass of water.

"You can make one of those caps easily. Just buy one rubber glove at the ten-cent store, fit it over a glass, tie it tightly with string above the rim, and cut off the rest of the hand and the fingers. Then you're all set."

Operator 5 turned away, seeing his father gazing at the black headlines on the newspapers. Ex-Operator Q-6 exclaimed: "It's appalling the amount of oil that can be destroyed by the sabotage of one well! There are wells burning now in every field in the country—thousands of barrels of oil going up in smoke every hour while we need every drop of it!"

"The most merciless *saboteurs* in the world are working against us on land and sea, Dad!" Operator 5 declared. "I tell you, we're in a trap—and every minute it's closing down on us more tightly!"

He strode to the telephone and his eyes shone dark. He called the secret number of headquarters KT; and when he had exchanged signals, Z-7's voice carried over the wire. Operator 5 asked quickly:

"Reports, Chief?"

Z-7 MOANED. "Report after report of more sabotage in our oil-fields and on the ocean! We have still not received a gallon of crude oil from abroad since the destructive operations began. Aside from this, we have scarcely any progress to report. Our laboratory is working now to analyze Yerian's solvent gas but we can scarcely hope for any result. The most encouraging find is that one of Yerian's drums contains a fuel more powerful than any other, yet refined from petroleum.

"I have rushed the tests of that fuel. It is a gasoline of a highly superior type. The lab chemists believe that Yerian's reclaimed oil, coming as it does from cellular crevices underground, is of a different consistency than oil obtained by the usual flush method. It is apparently capable of being refined into a gasoline of remarkable power. One of our men insists that this new fuel will, with proper carburetion, give power to the extent of above three hundred miles per gallon—better than the new fuel recently hinted at in the press but which we know now exists in fact."

"Lord, Chief!" Operator 5 exclaimed. "That means the fuel supply of the United States, if ever Yerian's method is put into general use, will be increased not merely up to two hundred times, but up to four thousand! It will give the United States an unequaled advantage in the world of oil! We are facing an alternative of utter destruction or unrivaled supremacy!"

"Yes! And still everything depends upon our learning Yerian's secret. Until now, the airplanes searching for his gyro report no results. I have every available man hunting on the ground also. If any other lead is unearthed, we'll make quick work of it!" Jimmy Christopher went on solemnly: "I advise you to warn our defenses in the Panamá Canal Zone to maintain a constant vigilance against a possible attack."

"The Canal! Do you believe some enemy nation will try to disable it?"

"The destruction of the canal will be the first move of any attack directed against us, Chief. It is unsafe at this very moment, with that unknown submarine lurking in the Gulf. We know already that the Canal Zone is surrounded by the land-holdings of other nations who realize only too well its strategic value.* We cannot be too watchful!"

"I will warn the War Department at once!"

"Ring me again, Chief, the moment there is a new lead on either Yerian or Coronza!"

Jimmy Christopher turned away from the telephone slowly, his fingers strayed to the golden ornament of death dangling from his watch-chain. He was reaching for his coat when a jangle of the telephone brought him brusquely to the instrument. The voice that spoke was Diane Elliot's.

"Jimmy! I'm watching Professor Yerian's home now. The men I relieved told me that no one has come or gone for hours—

---

* AUTHOR'S NOTE: It is startling to know that Great Britain controls great tracts of land adjacent to the Panamá Canal. British Controlled Oilfields, Ltd., is an agency of the British government and has leased lands in Guatemala, Honduras, Costa Rica, Nicaragua, British Guinea, Panamá, Venezuela, Colombia, Ecuador, Peru and Trinidad. None of these lands produces much oil, but they are centered around the vital waterway belonging to the United States. A shrewd French observer has declared that these encircling properties were chosen on both the Atlantic and the Pacific expressly as a precaution in case of war between Great Britain and the United States—as refueling stations.

what I have just seen may mean nothing, but—a telegram has just been delivered."

"Good! Don't take your eyes from that house, Di!"

"I won't! I don't know what the message says, Jimmy, but I'm gambling that it may be from the professor, and if it is—I'll do my best to spot him!"

"Good girl! 'Phone KT, Di, the moment you pick up the thread!"

"Jimmy!" The girl's voice rose with excitement "A car is stopping in front of the house now—a light coupé! There's a garage man in it. He's going to the door. I—I'll call back later!"

The connection clicked off as a bright new light began to shine in Operator 5's eyes....

CHAPTER 9
BLACK TRAP

DIANE ELLIOT slipped breathlessly from the telephone-booth, ran to the door of the corner drugstore. Through the panes, she had been able to watch the Yerian home while telephoning Operator 5. She hastened into the street—Broadway, weirdly deserted of automobiles—and turned toward the even greater quiet of Riverside Drive. Midway in the block sat the brownstone house she had been watching for an hour.

She walked past, while the man in coveralls waited at the front door. She saw the entrance open; a girl looked out. The girl, Diane had learned on her previous visit to the Yerian home, was the professor's daughter, Doré. As the garage man handed the ignition key to her, Diane heard him remark:

"You're lucky to have a little gas left. My pump's dry. This is the only car I've taken out today."

Diane glanced back as the man in coveralls walked away. She turned quickly, was retreating into the shadow of a doorway when she saw a flutter of movement at a dark window above the entrance. Someone was peering into the street from a lightless room—searching, Diane felt sure, for anyone who might be on watch. She waited until the curtain dropped back; then, quickly, she crossed the street.

She crouched behind the coupé, her mind racing. She had no car; she could not possibly follow this one when it started off. Her only alternative was, if possible, to go with it. She watched the windows intently as she turned the handle of the rumble compartment. She opened it, sprang up. She hid herself hastily in the dark hollow in front of the seat and lowered the cover. She tucked one of her gloves into the crack to keep the catch from springing into its socket and making her a helpless prisoner.

In utter darkness she waited there. Each second seemed endless; the air was heavy. She strained her ears to hear every slightest sound. She was startled, suddenly, by a slight swaying of the car. Someone had stepped on the running-board. A door clacked shut; and the snarl of the starter sounded. Jubilantly, Diane Elliot assured herself that no one had seen her enter the car; but she knew definitely that someone was leaving the Yerian home in response to the message she had seen delivered.

The vibration of the exhaust drummed in the girl's ears as

the coupé started off. Crouched uncomfortably in the darkness, Diane braced herself as the car turned. She realized she was now traveling north on Riverside Drive. The car stopped, went on, stopped again, turned and again turned. The girl in the rumble compartment conjectured that the driver was circling back in an effort to shake off anyone who might be following. Only slight precaution was necessary, because any other car in motion was immediately noticeable. The speed of the coupé increased.

Diane Elliot dared not raise the cover of the rumble-seat in order to learn her surroundings, but she felt that the car was climbing a steady incline. Suddenly brakes slowed it. Diane heard the tinkle of coins, deduced that the driver was paying toll to cross the George Washington bridge. A gruff voice sounded:

"The gas you're usin' up is mighty valuable right now, miss. The government needs it. How do I know you're not wastin' it when one of our army airplanes ought to have it?"

A girl's voice answered: "I—I've been saving this tank full because I've been expecting an important message. My sister is seriously ill in Newark. This telegram has just called me there."

After a pause, the gruff voice rumbled: "I guess it's okay. Go on. But you better not run out of gas gettin' there, because you won't be able to buy any more."

DIANE ELLIOT smiled to herself as the car spurted up. Her investigation of the Yerian family had taught her that the scientist had only one daughter—therefore Doré Yerian could have no sister. The message that had satisfied the patrolman revealed to Diane that the wording carried a disguised meaning. Her hope that it was from Professor Yerian mounted—hope that the scientist's daughter had been summoned to some secret rendezvous with him.

The coupé rolled on—and to Diane, the distance seemed interminable. Baffling turns followed each other until she was completely lost. Presently, she sensed that the car was slowing; she felt it turn carefully. It jounced over rough ground, swung again, and stopped. The girl hidden in the rumble compartment heard a husky voice order as the motor hummed off:

"Close the garage doors, Doré—at once!"

Diane Elliot's heart speeded. The car swayed again; footfalls sounded; rusty hinges squeaked. A second door closed; a bolt rattled into its socket. Waiting breathlessly, Diane listened. At last she ventured to lift the lid of the compartment; she raised her head into cold darkness and took a deep breath.

Thick gloom filled the garage. The only light was a white line shining beneath the door in the side wall—the door that had been fastened. Beyond it voices were speaking—one that of Doré Yerian, the other a man's. Diane Elliot climbed down carefully and crept close while the man declared huskily:

"I cannot stay here long! There have been airplanes flying overhead; I'm afraid the autogyro may be seen from the air. I was obliged to go out for food and a foreign-looking man, sitting in a car, saw me—followed me! I think I threw him off, but it's dangerous to stay. Unless I can find a safer place, they may kill me!"

"But—" The girl's voice spoke hesitantly. "Where can you go, father? How can you get away?"

"I can disguise myself a little. I can get back to New York and book passage on some coal-burning boat. I must get out of the country, Doré, as soon as possible! I need money. I have none with me and I dare not get it myself. You must get the money as soon as the bank opens in the morning. Mail it to me under Orth's name in care of General Delivery at the Central Post Office in New York. I intend to go as far as possible from this country—and before I leave, I'll destroy my data!"

"Father! You have spent your life—!"

"I will lose my life because of it unless I escape at once! I will not permit my process to be used to obtain fuel for war machines! I will not let—Listen!"

The voice stopped abruptly; Diane Elliot's heart speeded. A moment of silence followed while she poised motionless in the gloom. Professor Yerian's voice came again at last, a whisper.

"I thought I heard a sound outside! I'm afraid this house is being watched. That man who followed me—!"

Again, silence. Quickly, Diane Elliot crept along the wall to the deeper darkness in the corner of the garage. She heard Yerian moving about; she pictured him shifting from window to window, listening, peering out. She crouched behind the front of the coupé, breathing fast.... Then, at last, the voices resumed, tense and whispering. Diane Elliot peered at the car while Yerian's words rang in her mind:

"I must get out of the country as soon as possible! Before I leave I'll destroy my data!"

DIANE ROSE. With the utmost care, she loosened the spring catches of the hood of the car. Straining to make no noise, she lifted the hood, groped to the distributor head. She pried the clamps loose carefully. Her heart pounded with anxiety as she twisted off the arm of the distributor. Quickly then she replaced the cap, lowered the hood, and clamped it. With the vital part held in one small fist, she retreated again to the corner.

She heeled dirt loose at the edge of a can that had held oil. She put the distributor arm in the hollow and buried it. She moved the can carefully to cover the loose earth. Her lips twirked with triumph as she stole away. Without the distributor-arm, she knew, the coupé could not be moved. Without the car, Professor Yerian and his daughter must remain here; Yerian's departure must be delayed. Delayed, she hoped, until she could telephone headquarters KT—until Operator 5 could come!

At the outer door, she loosened the latch. Somewhere near, she felt sure, she could find a telephone. Once she flashed word to KT, Jimmy Christopher could reach this place almost immediately. Once—Diane Elliot's heart froze. From the rusted hinges of the garage door, a dry, piercing rasp issued.

"What's that?"

Professor Yerian's voice crackled inside the room beyond. Instantly a bolt snapped. Frantically, Diane flung the garage open as a stream of light fell from the door opening in the side wall. Professor Yerian, silhouetted against the glare, sprang through. Diane Elliot gasped and broke into a run. She sped into the open and Yerian's swift footfalls came after her.

The lean, spring-muscled scientist bounded closer. He flung one arm around the girl's waist; he slapped his other hand across her mouth. As his desperate strength dragged her back, she squirmed and kicked desperately to free herself. Her teeth sank into the flesh of Yerian's hand, but he did not release her. Her sharp heels drove at his legs, but he pulled her into the darkness of the garage. He flung her through the open door and she stumbled in the glare of a brightly lighted room.

She brought herself up; whirled back to find Professor Yerian leveling a revolver at her—a gun that glinted no less brightly, no less coldly, than his eyes.

Diane Elliot's breath beat hotly; her eyes snapped with anger. "You can't stop me! I'm leaving! I dare you to shoot me!"

She started for the door; and Yerian shifted swiftly to block her way. The dangerous gleam of his eyes had deepened. The girl paused, chilled by their bitter fury and their merciless determination. Yerian's voice rasped: "If you try to leave this place I'll kill you!"

Diane's chin rose defiantly. "You don't understand!" she tried to explain. "You won't be harmed because I've found you here. I'm acting for the United States government, and I promise you—"

"I want no promises from your government!" Professor Yerian snapped. "I loathe this government! I detest anyone connected with it! You have not saved yourself by saying that!"

Diane's eyes did not flinch. "What do you intend to do with me, then?" she demanded. "If you—"

"I intend to keep you prisoner here. You'll stay here until I am far outside this country. By that time, the data of my process will no longer exist. You came here to learn the secret—I know! You think that I will turn my process over to the United States government so that it can be saved from destruction! I will do nothing of the sort. I am going to keep the secret of my process and watch this government be wiped off the face of the earth!"

Diane declared: "You will see exactly that unless—"

"Exactly that—yes! Your government threw me into prison. Your government forced me to suffer dishonor as a convict. The matter of a few dollars—the federal taxes I failed to pay—seemed very great to it then! The matter of oil supply seems ever greater now—doesn't it? Yes! Now it is my turn!"

Diane recoiled from the blazing hatred shining in the eyes of Professor Yerian.

"THE MONEY I should have paid to the government—I falsified my returns and kept it because I needed it to perfect my process! Throwing me into prison delayed me years—cost me dearly. And now you expect me to hand that process over to the government!" Yerian's voice rang with bitter scorn. "Had they not made a convict of me I would have done so—gladly. I should have acted in the name of patriotism to the United States. Now I acknowledge no such allegiance. Now it is my hour—and I'll be glad to see your damnable government annihilated!"

Diane Elliot said quietly, coldly: "You hold in your hands the power to save the United States and you refuse—?"

"I refuse to save it! All the money in the world, all the power that can be turned upon me, will not induce me to reveal my process to any foreign government—nor to the United States!"

Professor Yerian reached behind him. He twisted a key in the lock of the door. He shifted across the room, keeping his revolver leveled at Diane Elliot. His voice rasped again:

"Keep back, Doré. You must not endanger yourself. Do you hear?"

Doré Yerian, her bright eyes alight with anxiety, her red lips parted, retreated to the side of the room. Her father reached for the knob of a door behind Diane. He jerked it open, revealing a closet. He faced the girl grimly and his revolver pressed to her body.

"Back up! I will not hesitate to kill you if you give me cause. No human being in the world means anything to me now but my daughter. Back up, I say!"

Diane straightened. "Professor Yerian," she said coldly, "you are about to become the greatest traitor in all the United States history."

"I cannot be a traitor to a government I long ago disavowed!… You back into that closet, or—"

Diane's eyes hashed. She turned grimly; she strode into the closet. Instantly Professor Yerian closed the door upon her. Utter darkness surrounded her as the key grated in the lock. Heavy footfalls sounded beyond, and Yerian's voice penetrated the panels harshly:

"Doré! You must go at once! It is dangerous for you here! I no longer care what they do to me, but—you must not be harmed. I would rather sacrifice my data than endanger you. Go—now!"

Lighter footfalls crossed the floor, and Diane Elliot knew that the girl was hurrying into the garage. She heard the starter of the coupé grind—and grind again. Her lips began to tighten wryly as Yerian's dismayed words carried to her, as the girl voiced breathless concern. Several times again the gears snarled and the motor of the coupé failed to catch.

"Something's wrong, father! The car won't start!"

With grim pleasure, Diane Elliot listened to the continued efforts of the girl and the scientists to revive the motor. Their attempts continued while the battery of the coupé weakened—until, at last, the starter would no longer turn. Professor Yerian snarled his fury as he returned to the inner room.

"I can't get back now, father!" the girl exclaimed. "You won't be able to leave the country now! You've got to stay here—and I'm going to stay with you!"

"No, Doré!"

"I'm going to stay!"

"But it's dangerous! I know this place is being watched! Doré—stay away from that door. Go into the next room—lock it. If anyone comes in here, if anyone tries to harm you now, I'll kill him on the spot!"

Quick footfalls crossed the floor—the girl's. Diane Elliot heard a connecting door close, heard a key twist in a lock. She sensed Yerian's quick breathing; she could picture him watching the entrance with leveled gun. Her hands felt walls she could not see. She knew she was securely imprisoned. Her eyes stung with bitter tears as she realized there was no way—no possible way now—of reaching Operator 5....

CHAPTER 10
CANNED DOOM

A T THE stage entrance of the grimy, lightless Knicker-bocker Theatre, Jimmy Christopher paused. He spoke in a whisper to the man lounging in the doorway: "Refinery A." He slipped through the door when it opened. He code-worded his way past another sentry; he trod along a row of dressing-rooms at the rear of the theatre; he thrust into Z-7's office.

The Washington chief sprang up, seized his hand. "I am afraid that we are finding ourselves in a hopeless situation. These reports—" Z-7 gestured wearily toward a heap of flimsies scattered over his desk. "More sabotage! More wells going up in flame! Two more refineries destroyed by explosions! Still not a drop of petroleum has reached our shores from abroad! Industry is paralyzed; normal life has ceased to exist. We are doing everything possible, and yet we are making no headway."

Dark lines deepened around Operator 5's eyes. "I will not admit the situation is hopeless, Chief. It is certainly the most dangerous crisis we have ever faced—but we're not through, by any means. From the airplanes searching for Yerian's gyro—any reports, Chief?"

"Reports, yes—but no results!" Z-7 turned quickly as a shirt-sleeved agent hurried from the dispatcher's room.

His eyes were widened; he was breathless. He blurted: "Chief! An SOS coming in! Just picked it up! A ship in distress!"

The Washington chief uttered an expression of dismay as he strode through the connecting door. Jimmy Christopher followed him into the room where the wireless equipment of KT was functioning. A man hunched at a panel, 'phones clamped to his ears, gestured them to two other pairs lying on the table. Operator 5 and Z-7 put them on. Through the ether they heard the piping note of a transmitter sending code rapidly. The dots and dashes formed themselves swiftly into a pattern of words!

SOS—SOS—SOS—Tanker Rebound approaching New Orleans—sea pouring in—ship sinking rapidly—struck by a torpedo—

"Torpedo!" Z-7 snapped. "Good God! That damned submarine was last seen in the Gulf and now—!"

The whining note sang again in the 'phones: *—Crew abandoning ship—sea breaking over deck—cannot remain at post much longer—First Officer reported sighting submarine few minutes following explosion—sub has now disappeared—ship listing heavily—going down—*

Z-7 PEERED haggardly at Operator 5 as the oscillator note stuttered—and disappeared. That meant that the wireless operator on the distressed ship had been forced to abandon his key. The ether now was tensely silent, and the silence blanketed an appalling disaster hundreds of miles away, a tragedy on the night sea. Jimmy Christopher slipped off his 'phones slowly:

"The one tanker we knew was close to port—the one supply of oil we were counting on, going to the bottom of the sea!" Z-7 rose, his face white. "Sinking that ship is an act of war—by an unknown nation! A deliberate attack!"

Jimmy Christopher turned away, his fingers straying to the golden death-charm on his watch-chain—but an exclamation from a second wireless operator arrested his attention.

"A report coming in from one of the patrolling airplanes! Get it!"

Jimmy Christopher again fitted 'phones to his ears. Through a rumble of static, a voice penetrated. From some point in the distant sky, the observer of an army airplane was speaking through the ether.

"Calling KT! Olds in Four-Five-One reporting! I have spotted a plane partly hidden beneath trees directly below! The light of the rising sun has just struck it! I'm using binoculars and I'm sure it's a gyro!"

Jimmy Christopher brought the microphone close to his lips. "We've got you, Four-Five-One! Give me the location of that craft at once! Stay directly above it!"

Operator 5's pencil flew as the observer in the far-away sky spoke again. "The field is west of Palisades Park. There is a small house on it. There are woods all around. The Hudson-Hilldale Road passes near it. Turn right off the Washington Bridge— approximately twelve miles. You can spot the house—a corrugated roof with garage adjoining!"

"Hold it!" Jimmy Christopher snapped. "Remain directly above that point—keep circling. You will see cars approaching soon and you're to guide us from the air. Remain there after we arrive and wait for further orders!"

"Gyro still directly below!"

Jimmy Christopher snapped off the 'phones. He strode swiftly into Z-7's office. There the Washington chief was speaking ringingly into a telephone.

"General McBride, the General Staff must meet the emergency of the submarine lurking in the Gulf! Issue new orders at once to the Coast Guard and our naval scouts! Find that damned sub! You've got to find it, sir, before it drives a torpedo into the Panamá Canal locks—before that waterway is crippled!"

Operator 5 snapped as Z-7 broke the connection with the Chief of Staff in Washington: "We've spotted Yerian's gyro! We're going to that field as fast as we can get there! Let's go, Chief!"

He jerked out the door and his heels hammered hard....

THE RISING sun shafted golden light across the road skirting behind the Palisades, parallel with the broad Hudson—a road empty save for two cars that sped northward with wide-open throttles. They were Intelligence machines; their precious fuel was devoted to the service of the United States government. Operator 5 drove the first.

Z-7, beside him, bent forward tensely, listening to a surging voice carrying from the radio bracketed under the dash. The sensitive receiver was tuned to the wavelength used by the patrolling airplanes; distorters were in operation in both plane and car, making it impossible for any other listener-in to intercept the vital messages. The voice of Olds, in Four-Five-One twanged:

"I've spotted you on the road! The next left turn leads to the field where the gyro is hidden. Wait! Careful! Don't take that turn yet! Another car is approaching from the opposite direction!"

Z-7 snapped into the sedan's short-wave transmitter: "What! That car is not an Intelligence machine. Watch it!"

"I've got it spotted! It's moving slowly, apparently making no attempt to hide its movements. It's literally crawling along. Now it's swinging to the side of the road and stopping. It's still almost a mile from the field. The driver is apparently waiting for someone."

Operator 5 brought the microphone close to his lips as he drove. "Can we reach that house without being sighted by the other car?"

"Yes! There's a dead-end road in the woods—the second turn left. Take it as far as you can through the woods in a course perpendicular to the road. You'll come out opposite the house."

Operator 5 pressed the accelerator. He spurted past the first turn, swung into the second. The car jounced over rough dirt. Tight brakes stopped it where the road ended. Jimmy Christopher ducked out as the second Intelligence machine pulled up behind. He peered skyward through bare branches; far above, soundless; the patrolling plane was a mere dot in the sky.

Z-7 and four Intelligence operators came immediately to Jimmy Christopher's side. He led the way through the woods, working toward the other road. When he paused, he was within sight of a small house sitting isolated at the edge of a spreading field. Behind it drawn as far as possible beneath a clump of trees, sat an autogyro, its prop still, its vane drooping. Operator 5 signaled caution.

"Z-7, cross the road with me. I'm going into that house. You men are to stay out of sight, on this side of the road. If that other car comes, wait to see what the driver intends to do. If anyone leaves it to go into that house, let him; then take possession of the car and make prisoners of anyone in it. Watch sharp!"

Jimmy Christopher stepped cautiously into the open. He and Z-7 crossed the space in front of the house. Operator 5 drew close to the Washington chief and whispered: "Stay out of sight behind the garage. If anyone comes in from the car, shift to the door and keep him in."

Jimmy Christopher sped soundlessly to the opposite side of the house as Z-7 darted to the rear of the garage. The long shadows of the rising sun covered him as he paused at a window and listened. He heard a husky voice speaking inside and his eyes sharpened.

"We cannot risk staying here longer! We've got to get back— on foot if there is no other way. I tell you we must!"

A GIRL'S low voice answered with words which Operator 5 could not distinguish. He shifted quietly to the rear of the house. At another window, he stooped, peering beneath the edge of a drawn blind to see a small bedroom beyond. He tried the sash and found it fastened. From his hip pocket he drew a thin tool of steel, its sharp edge fish-tailed. He pried into the crack and bore down with all his strength.

Bit by bit, his lever pulled the screws of the catch from the dry wood. The sash tore loose. Noiselessly Operator 5 raised it. He legged over the sill quickly; he darted to a closed door. Through the panels he heard the husky voice again.

"Now, Doré—now! We cannot stay here; we must go! I am ready! But before I pass out that door I'm going to make sure that no despotic government ever comes into possession of my records!"

Jimmy Christopher's fingers twined hard to the knob of the door. He twisted it without sound; he drew it open slowly, peered through the crack. On the opposite side of the room he saw a girl standing, back turned; she was watching a lean, gaunt-faced man who had turned to the wall. Professor Norton Yerian was removing books from a built-in case. A red glow played upon him as he spilled the volumes aside—a shine from the open door of a stove standing against the wall. A bed of live coals lay within it. Yerian, working beside it, reached to the wall space he had cleared. He pressed, and a square section yielded; he thrust it aside to disclose a cavity. From the hiding-place, he removed a large, thick, brown envelope, sealed with red wax.

He turned quickly with it to the open door of the stove, his back still turned to Operator 5. The girl watched him in silent fascination as he tore the flap of the envelope open, as he fingered the papers it contained.

"The only copy of my data in all the world!" he exclaimed breathily. "Data that any nation in the world would pay a king's ransom for! Information that would make the United States the supreme power in the world of oil. My life's work! In a moment it will be nothing but ashes!"

He thrust the precious papers toward the sparkling coals. Instantly, Operator 5 snapped the door open. His voice rang sharply into the hush:

"One moment!"

Professor Yerian whirled, his eyes blazing, his fingers tightened white around the envelope. Doré Yerian recoiled, her hand flying to her red lips to suppress a cry. Man and daughter stood motionless, startled and frozen, as Jimmy Christopher took slow strides into the room, grim determination on his face.

"I cannot permit you, Professor Yerian, to destroy that data!"

Yerian straightened. His hand moved again, quickly toward the open door of the stove—the hand gripping the envelope. With lightning swiftness, Jimmy Christopher's hand darted inside his coat. It blurred and came level, pointing an automatic straight at the scientist. Operator 5's voice took on a sharper edge.

"Wait!… The last thing in the world I wish, Professor Yerian, is to harm you. You deserve respect as one of the greatest scientists living. But you know that the fate of my government is hanging in the balance at this moment. I warn you that I will take any means to prevent your destroying your report!"

YERIAN'S HAND paused. Suddenly a thumping sound echoed in the room. It startled Operator 5, but his gun did not waver, his eyes did not flick from the scientist's haggard face. The knocking came from a door at his right and a muffled voice called—a girl's: "Jimmy! Jimmy Christopher!"

"Diane!"

The name burst from Operator 5's lips. Swiftly he stepped aside. Without his glance leaving Yerian's smouldering eyes, he groped to the knob of the door and twisted the key. At once, it flew open. Diane Elliot stepped out and paused, pale, breathless. Operator 5's gaze darkened as his free hand sought hers.

"Good girl! You found him, didn't you, Di! Steady, now!"

Instantly, Coronza's
automatic blazed at
Professor Yerian!

"Jimmy!" the girl blurted. "I know why he refuses to give the data to the United States government. It's because the government jailed him—because he falsified his tax reports in order to get more money to carry on his oil experiments."

Operator 5 straightened. "Professor Yerian, you cannot insist upon the extinction of the United States government as revenge for any injustice you have suffered. You cannot go so far as to destroy those who are not responsible for your imprisonment. This does not mean the end of the government alone. It means that millions of families—men like yourself, women like the mother of your daughter, girls like her—will be forced into abject slavery under the dictatorship of a militaristic machine."

Yerian straightened. "They have all—all of them been victimized in the world struggle for oil! The sooner all oil disappears from the face of the earth, the better—if it is to be used to feed machines of war!"

"The United States is thinking only of defense against machines of war, sir!"

The scientist snarled. "You cannot alter my decision! I am going to destroy this data—now! If you mean to kill me in order to stop me—you will find it necessary to act at once!"

Yerian's hand thrust the precious document to the open door of the stove—into the scorching heat of the coals. Operator 5's forefinger trembled on the trigger of the automatic. His eyes challenged those of Professor Yerian.

One slight move of the scientist's hand, he realized, would drop the precious document into the shimmering coals. Once they fell on the white-hot bed, the terrific heat would destroy

140

them in a few moments. Yerian stood motionless, hand extended, gripping the sheaf of papers, his darkened face a threat. Slowly, Jimmy Christopher took a step toward him.

The grim glitter of Operator 5's eyes held the scientist spellbound. Again he stepped forward, while Yerian stood fascinated. The leaves covered with invaluable data curled in the radiating heat as he advanced carefully. Into Yerian's eyes a desperate light sprang as Operator 5's hand began to reach toward his. Jimmy Christopher's fingers neared the sheaf of documents and the scientist tensed.

Suddenly Yerian jerked the data out of Operator 5's reach—flung the sheaf into the stove!

"It's burning! Burning!"

Desperately, swiftly, Jimmy Christopher thrust his hand into the terrific heat. The pack of papers had fallen onto the center of the bed of coals; flame was bursting from it. The sheets of priceless data were spurting out streamers of smoke. Operator 5's hand stung with the scorching heat as he reached to grasp the charring documents, to jerk them out.

A shot!

The bullet pinged from the doorway, followed instantly by the slap of the swinging door as it met the wall. A man sprang into the room the instant the slug slashed at Operator 5's wrist. Reflex action jerked Jimmy Christopher's hand back as the hot lead seared his skin. The roar of the report sent his hand flashing upward with his own automatic. He spun toward the man who had leaped into the room, and the guns of the two glittered into line.

"Don't touch that! Unless you wish to die—unless you wish everyone inside this house and outside it to die instantly—don't touch it!"

Coronza!

CHAPTER 11
DEATH IN A CAPSULE

JAIME CORONZA peered darkly at Operator 5—and deliberately, slowly lowered his gun. Jimmy Christopher quickly turned to the stove. While he covered Coronza, he reached again, desperately, toward the documents that were now flaming. And again Coronza spoke—spoke with a biting ring:

"Touch it, and you will die—the ladies with you, *Señor!*"

At Coronza's last word, a quick step sounded behind him. On the sill, Z-7 appeared, white-faced, his black eyes smouldering. Operator 5's hand had stopped short; his first swift glance, his first concern, was for Diane Elliot. His gaze shot again to Coronza. The espionage agent, he saw now, was holding a tin contained in his left hand; the fingers were curled through the handle. Z-7 paused, just inside the room, his lips trembling with a warning.

"That car!" he exclaimed in a rush of breath. "It's loaded with tins of nitroglycerine! The motor's running! The man at the wheel has it in gear, headed for the house. He defies—!"

Z-7 broke off, peering in horror at the container held loosely in Jaime Coronza's fingers. The espionage agent's evil smile had broadened. Into the hush that followed the Washington chief's words he spoke drawlingly:

"It is quite true. There is enough nitroglycerine in that can to blow up a city. A slight shock will set it off—as, for instance, if it strikes the front of this house. The can I am holding in my hand likewise contains nitroglycerines—one gallon. If I should drop it—" Coronza shrugged. "I have only to move my fingers slightly. The explosion will burst this house and kill everyone in it instantly. I shall drop this can, Operator 5, if you make another move to get those papers out of the fire!"

Jimmy Christopher peered in agony into the Spaniard's ugly face. His gaze shot to the documents lying on the coals—precious papers now disappearing into ash. Again his glance turned wretchedly to Diane Elliot.

Z-7 BLURTED: "There's no doubt of it, Operator 5! Remember how that car crawled so carefully over this road! The driver has four guns on him now, and he refuses to obey commands. He has only to let the clutch back and the car will spurt toward this house!"

The fire raging within the stove gleamed on Operator 5's face. He stared past Z-7 into the road. Directly in front of the house, outside the gate, a sedan was sitting. It was the car which Five-Four-One had seen creeping around bumps and hollows. On its rear seat, gleaming tin cans were piled high—containers like that one held now so loosely in Jaime Coronza's fingers. Four Intelligence agents were straddled around it, leveling their guns at the man at the wheel. His dark face was lined with an ugly, triumphant grimace. The motor of his sedan was racing.

"It is not a bluff!" Z-7 exclaimed. "If we put a bullet in that man, the clutch will catch—the car will drive against the house. That will be enough to set off the explosive. There is nothing we can do—nothing! For God's sake, obey Coronza!"

Operator 5's lips tightened as he peered at the swarthy espionage agent.

"Your gun is trained straight at me," Coronza remarked. "A pull on the trigger will kill me. Yet, of course, if you shot I would drop this container. There would be no trace left of this house or of any of us! I suggest that you remain exactly where you are. From your position, you will be able to watch the last of the data sheets burn until nothing but ash remains!"

Jimmy Christopher's face went white with suppressed fury as he heard Coronza's sneering words. A choking cry sounded behind him: "Doré!"

Professor Yerian's daughter turned in terror; she ran to her father. Operator 5 turned to see the scientist's arms tighten anxiously around her as he peered fearfully at Coronza.

"For God's sake—let her go!" Yerian pleaded. "Let her leave this house! She has done nothing—!"

"She remains!" Jaime Coronza's voice grew edged. "You will all do exactly as I say. At the slightest disobedience, I will drop this can. I am ready to pay my life in the service of the Great Entente. I should prefer death here to—a firing-squad and a stone wall!"

Operator 5 felt, in spite of the agony of the moment, admiration for the Spaniard's coolness. He glanced again into the hot heart of the stove, saw that now the precious documents were destroyed beyond all possible reclamation—documents recording a secret upon which the existence of a great nation depended! He glanced up haggardly as Coronza strode to the open entrance.

"Partoni! We will be leaving at once, *amigo mío!*"

Z-7 strode swiftly toward the sedan as the man at the wheel moved. Partoni raised his hand—a hand loosely holding one of the cans of doom. Raising it high, by the tips of his fingers, he disengaged the gears, opened the door, and slipped from the seat. The guns of the four Intelligence men jerked—but Partoni's triumphant smile widened. "Do not interfere with me!" he warned.

STILL HOLDING the one container, he opened the rear of the car and reached for another. He handled it gently, avoiding any possible jar, as Z-7's face went white. Partoni placed the second can on the ground beside the car. He removed another and another until he formed a row; and, calmly, still holding the first, he began placing more cans on the tops of the line! While the Washington chief watched in helpless horror, the espionage agent coolly built a pyramid of explosive!

In the doorway Coronza watched. He had calmly turned his back toward Operator 5's gun. He strode back into the room, his teeth gleaming again through an evil smile.

"Do you understand?" he asked suavely. "This pile of cans forms an easy target, visible far down the road—no? A bullet fired into one of them will explode them all. *Por Dios*, Partoni is an expert marksman! He has a powerful rifle with him now. When we leave, Partoni's rifle will be aimed at the stack of containers. If you attempt to give chase! Ah! I see you comprehend!"

Coronza advanced with an insolent swagger. "Señor Operator 5, you are a very dangerous adversary—yet now you must know that your game is lost. I came here with the intention, señor, of taking the data for myself, but I am satisfied with the second best thing—to see it completely destroyed. Your country lies absolutely powerless before the Great Entente. Bow to my superior shrewdness, *Señor!*"

Coronza's dark eyes shifted to Professor Yerian and blazed. His free hand swung slowly to his hip pocket. He raised it, gripping a huge automatic. Yerian's face went colorless as the gigantic weapon gleamed at him. The Spaniard's voice raised to call out the door: "Partoni! Have you finished?"

"Ready!"

"Into the other car, then!" Coronza spoke through tight lips. "You understand fully that attempting to stop me now, attempting to follow us, will mean your destruction—instantly! Very well! Before I leave, I will assure myself that your one last possible means of learning the secret of the Yerian process—dies!"

Instantly Coronza's automatic blazed—swiftly—three times! Thrice lead lightning struck across the room. Operator 5 leaped into Coronza's line of fire as the reports blended into one shocking burst—but the swiftness of the spy's move completed it before Jimmy Christopher's fastest nervous reaction could stop it. Operator 5 whirled, his dark eyes blazing, his automatic leveled, facing Coronza at a spot across which the bullets had flashed.

A choking cry came from behind him. He glanced back once swiftly, to see Professor Yerian staggering—clutching at his chest, dropping on sagging knees. Three slugs had torn into the body of the scientist—slugs fired with such speed that no man could have prevented the attack. A scream tore from Doré Yerian as her father lurched to the floor and lay still.

"Back!" Coronza warned ringingly. Remember, *por Dios!* One slight movement of my finger and—!"

THE HUGE automatic in Coronza's hand jerked toward Doré Yerian. She saw the glitter and recoiled in speechless terror. Operator 5 moved swiftly—moved directly in front of Coronza's gun. He stepped between the espionage agent and the girl with his own weapon leveled.

Jimmy Christopher's lips began to twirk into a wry smile. "You know that if you pull that trigger, our bullets will cross. You will die as quickly as I. You will not live to see the Great Entente conquer the United States.... Are you going to shoot, Coronza?"

A jerk of Coronza's hand swung the heavy container. His eyes glittered with a vicious light. "I have achieved my purpose," he declared throatily. "I have made it certain that the United States be doomed. I prefer to live to witness the fruits of my success. Between you and me, Operator 5—stalemate! Yet—*por Dios!*—do not dare try to follow me!"

Operator 5 stood rigid as Coronza backed to the door. Beyond, in the road, Partoni was still holding the dread container; but in his other hand now he had raised a long-range rifle. In calm defiance of the guns of the Intelligence agents, he turned away, striding toward a second car which was parked beyond—a roadster with its top down. He climbed to the seat, raised the rifle, aimed it deliberately at the stack of nitroglycerine cans, and called: "Ready, Coronza!"

In the doorway, Coronza peered coldly at Jimmy Christopher. "Operator 5, I consider you my most dangerous enemy. I intend to make sure that your danger to me ends now. *Now, señor!*"

Coronza backed through the door; he strode away. Jimmy Christopher grimly and quickly followed. He snapped orders to the Intelligence men: "Let them go!"

Z-7 watched in cold fury as Coronza climbed to the wheel of the roadster. The Spaniard held the container of explosive with extended arm, beyond the door of the car, as he started the motor and sent the wheels rolling.

The roadster sped. Braced above the seat, Partoni kept the rifle leveled at the stack of cans beside the abandoned car. Through the thin dust that rose, his steadied rifle glinted in the morning sun. Z-7 exclaimed breathily: "Don't move! Stand where you are until they are out of sight!"

Suddenly, as the roadster whirled down the road, Operator 5 saw Partoni swing the rifle—swing it directly toward him! Fire flashed from the barrel the instant Jimmy Christopher leaped. The slug whined past him, fanning his cheek with its hot breath, as he bounded again. He glimpsed Partoni's rifle turning back to the cans of nitroglycerine—and Operator 5 leaped directly in front of them.

Paralyzed, Z-7 saw Operator 5 wrench with a swift impact of power. He spun half around, arms out-thrown—and fell into the dust to lay still.

SCARCELY AWARE of his own movements, Z-7 sprang forward and glanced along the dust-clouded road. He saw Partoni's vague figure tottering. A gasp of relief broke from his lips as the man with the rifle sprawled forward, the weapon dropping from his hands. The espionage agent spilled head downward into the road, rolled violently, lurched into a rain-washed gully—as the car carrying Coronza veered from sight....

The Washington chief snatched at Operator 5's arm, turned him face up and saw a tear in his coat, directly above the heart—a tear made by the rifle-bullet. Operator 5's automatic had dropped Partoni from the car at the very instant Partoni's bullet had struck him in return. White-faced, frozen with consternation, Z-7 peered at Jimmy Christopher. A flicker of Operator 5's eyelids brought a sigh from his lips.

Jimmy Christopher dragged himself up confusedly, glancing swiftly around. He swayed to his feet, fumbled inside his coat while Z-7 peered—while the Intelligence operators hurried forward. From his inside pocket, Jimmy Christopher brought a square of silver, dented, wrenched out of shape by Partoni's bullet.

It was the case in which he carried his credentials signed by the President!

"Okay, Chief!" he exclaimed. "Coronza intended to kill me—to explode the cans after all!"

Z-7 stood transfixed, realizing that Partoni's bullet would have struck the containers of explosive except for Operator 5's swift action—and that Jimmy Christopher at this moment might have been lying dead in the dust of the road as a result.

149

Operator 5 steadied himself quickly, his breath coming fast, stepped from the pile of containers: "Get those cans back into the car! Run it out to the center of the field and guard it. Z-7— after me!"

He hurried into the room to find Doré Yerian bending frantically over her father, shaking his shoulders, sobbing. The scientist's shirt was sopping with blood; he lay limp and motionless. Operator 5 quickly knelt above him. His breath came slowly as he found a faint, irregular pulse. He jerked up as Z-7 came into the door and snapped:

"Get this man into your car, Chief—to a hospital as quickly as possible! He's dying. Stay with him! Diane, stick with the Chief!"

Z-7 paused to blurt: "The data! Are you positive it's completely destroyed?"

"Burned,—nothing but ashes!"

Operator 5 sped out the door. He bounded across the road, fought his way through the wood-lot to the Intelligence cars. He slipped swiftly to the front wheel of the second of them and checked the setting of the radio dials. He brought the microphone close to his lips and his voice rang sharply:

"Calling Five-Four-One! Calling Five-Four-One!" He pulled 'phones over his ears and listened—into silence. No voice answered his call. No response came from the sputtering ether. Again, imperatively, Jimmy Christopher sent his voice flashing into the sky.

"Calling Five-Four-One!"

CHAPTER 12
WARNING IN CODE

O UT OF the zenith an answer lightninged, distant, tremulous, but bell-clear: "Five-Four-One reporting!"

A sign burst past Operator 5's lips. "Olds! Are you still in position?"

"Yes! Directly above the field!"

"Do you see a car traveling over the road, away from the river?"

"Yes! I've been following it with my glasses!"

"Keep watching it!" Jimmy Christopher ordered. "Keep your eye on that car no matter where it goes! It's the most important detail you've ever had! Stay on the waveband! I'm depending absolutely on you to lead me after it!"

"I've got it!" Five-Four-One sang back. "Starting now!"

Operator 5, keeping the 'phones pressed to his ears, slipped behind the wheel. Quickly he backed the sedan, sent it streaking toward the main highway. He turned on whining tires and shot into the branch road. In a moment, he whizzed past the hidden house of Professor Yerian; his quick glance noticed the Intelligence men removing the cans of nitroglycerin with agonized carefulness. Static crackled in his ears as he sped on, and the voice of the observer in the sky carried down to him again.

"Turn right when you meet the pavement! That car is going like the wind, but I've still got it in the glasses! It's heading through the next town! Step on it!"

Operator 5 pushed the sedan's motor to the limit. He sped past the motionless body of Partoni, lying beside the road.

Reaching the end of the unpaved road, he swung sharply. In a moment, he was rushing through a suburb. Pedestrians stared as he passed. Jimmy Christopher ignored patrolmen who hurried from the curb to stop him, left them blinded by a whirling wind. Again open country lay ahead when the unseen observer overhead spoke again:

"Next left! You've gained on that car, but you can't get closer without being spotted. Steady! It's taking a sharp right turn into another suburb now.... It's heading through, slowing. Easy while I direct you!"

Painstakingly, Operator 5 followed the directions flashing to him. He left the center of the suburb behind him and turned upon a street which rapidly took on a sooty sordidness. Again Five-Four-One called:

"Now, straight ahead! You're four blocks from it! Third house from the corner on the fourth intersection, west side. Got it?"

"Got it!" Operator 5 repeated grimly. "Keep circling above! Watch on the chance that that car might leave again soon. If it does, follow it as long as your fuel supply lasts."

"We're good for hours yet! Okay!"

Operator 5 swung his car to the curb. He ducked out and walked hurriedly in the same direction. From the opposite side of the street, he gazed at the house which the observer had spotted. Beyond it, behind high fences, great painted tanks and thick pipes were visible—an oil refinery. At its closed gate, United States infantrymen were on guard. Grimly, Operator 5 realized that Coronza had deliberately selected an unlikely location for his hideaway. He strode briskly, observing the house through the corners of his eyes.

HE TURNED past the corner, rounded to the next street. The neighborhood was quiet except for the sounds of activity issuing from the enclosure of the guarded refinery. Jimmy Christopher strode through the yard of a drab house, approached the rear of that which Coronza had entered. Ducking behind the fence, he studied it, noted that the shade of every window was drawn tight.

He vaulted the fence, darted to the side of the house. Noiselessly, he slipped to the cellar-entrance. He tried it, found it immovable in its frame—nailed shut. He glided on, without sound, to a narrow basement window. He dropped to his knees, noted that the panes were painted black on the back side, and listened. No slightest noise reached him. He slipped from his pocket the tempered, steel tool with the fish tail edge.

He pried with painstaking caution, working the sharp edge deeper, levering against the window-catch. A snapping sound froze him. He listened with caught breath for a full moment; but no alarm arose. Easily he pushed the window inward on its hinges. He thrust his legs through, dropped, and turned with his automatic in his hand.

The basement was lightless, musty. Operator 5 pulled out his torch. Its narrow beam disclosed a flight of stairs at the far corner. He trod up them, listening at each step. At the top of the flight, he found a door—locked. Replacing the jimmy he drew out his pack of master-keys. Three times—each attempt made with consummate care—he tried before the bolt responded. He

153

Swift as the stroke of doom, with all the force of a rending

earthquake, the blast struck the room!

opened a crack; he slipped through; he stood in a dark hallway and heard voices.

The purring tones of Jaime Coronza were issuing from one of

the front rooms. Operator 5 crept closer, listening as he moved. He paused, pressed to the wall, as Coronza's voice rose:

"Is it not true that we secretly represent the greatest allegiance of statesmen in the world today? Is it not true that we have succeeded in our first great step—rendering the United States helpless, devoid of all oil supplies? Yes! Our next move must be made now! It will destroy once and for all the greatest danger we face now—the United States Intelligence Service!"

Operator 5 stood motionless, chilled by the confident ring of the espionage agent's declaration.

"First—" Coronza paused—"let us understand each other. We have served the Great Entente faithfully, at the risk of our lives. Our rewards will be rich. We represent, not nations, but factions within nations which are able, when we speak the word, to assume control of their respective governments. They await our signal. *Por Dios,* we are the pioneers of a great government still to be born—which will rise on the ruins of the United States!"

Jimmy Christopher moved forward again, slowly, soundlessly, straining to hear each word.

"Let their plan be carried out," Coronza continued, "but let us realize that ours will be a supreme power. We will be able secretly to control that government when it rises. Statesmen will do our bidding because we shall head the secret police, and the secret police will dominate. We shall become a council of rulers. *Madre de Dios,* there will be no power in the world greater than ours!"

Jimmy Christopher's gun steadied. He stepped forward, fingers tensed for the knob. He touched it, twisted it, and—

A sharp click sounded!

OPERATOR 5 sprang back instantly—yet the swiftness of his move was not enough to carry him clear of the crushing weight that dropped upon him. In a flash, he was struck on the head and shoulders by a clanking, grinding thing that whipped down to envelope his whole body. His gun was knocked downward. He staggered under the dazing power of the trap that had closed around him. Hurled to his knees, he struggled to rise against a force that pinioned him to the floor!

Coronza's voice snapped: "The door!"

Jimmy Christopher strove to rise as light flooded over him. He peered, stunned, to see shadow figures leaping through the swiftly opened door—men rushing to enclose him, guns in the hand of each. He thrust at the thing enveloping him, realized it was a huge snare of heavy, metal mesh. Interlocking steel links formed a blanket that had folded around him, a thing so weighty that no man could shake it off. Gasping, Jimmy Christopher sank back, seeing, through the fabric of steel, guns leveled at him.

Coronza exploded: "Again—Operator 5! *Por Dios!* Bring him in!"

The men surrounding Jimmy Christopher grasped the edges of the heavy veil of mesh. They groped in to grasp his arms and legs. His automatic was snatched away while he was still crushed to the floor. He was held helpless while the mesh was dragged free; he was jerked, dazed, to his feet. Bright light stung his eyes as he was thrust to the door.

He found himself at the head of a long table. Along both sides of it, men stood with guns leveled at him. At the far end, Jaime Coronza leaned forward tensely. Operator 5 straightened grimly. Coronza snapped at him:

"You are very clever to follow me here! You will remember I promised you death at our next meeting. Now I shall keep that promise!"

Operator 5 stood erect and cold, his dark eyes fixed sharply on the features of a man standing beside Coronza. Jimmy Christopher knew that man—a lieutenant of Z-7! Here, among international espionage agents who were scheming to destroy the United States government, stood a member of the United States Intelligence Service—the man designated R-9!

Into the silence of the room, Jimmy Christopher spoke ringingly: "I see that you have worked well, Coronza. You have turned one of our undercover agents against us. It is clear now why you have been informed of every step we have taken!"

R-9's square face went white; his eyes dropped. The others at the table kept their guns steadied at Operator 5, whose fingers strayed slowly to the little golden death-charm on his watch-chain.

"I recognize you all," he declared quietly, "as men without countries. Okato Hinzu, the undercover agent of a militaristic faction of Japan, plotting to overthrow his own government. Otto Slobel, once of the German Intelligence. Carlos Tierza, traitor to Italy, acting for an organized cabal against the dictator. Mr. Seaton Glave, formerly of the British Intelligence, now a spy for any nation willing to pay the prize. Perhaps, Mr. Glave, it was your intention to learn the secret of the Yerian process in order to sell it to the British Intelligence, who would in turn sell it to the Admiralty? I compliment you, gentlemen, on being as unscrupulous a group of men as ever assembled to threaten the peace of the world!"

Coronza sneered. "I suggest that you speak rapidly, Operator 5, for you have not much time to live!"

JIMMY CHRISTOPHER'S fingers toyed again with the

golden death-charm. They covered it from the sight of the other men. Carefully, he pressed upon a tiny concealed spring....

"We are, gentlemen," he said quietly, "facing a showdown. I know your plans—to wipe the United States government out of existence, to create a new imperialistic nation in its stead which you will rule with your organization of secret police. You are planning to let the nations which are waiting to invade these shores now fight among themselves for the spoils—then you will take command. You know my own purpose—to stop you at any cost!"

Coronza snapped: "Now you can do nothing. *Por Dios*, it is too late!"

Slowly Operator 5 smiled. "You men, here in this room," he declared, "are the real power threatening my country. Once you die, a great danger to the United States will be removed. You will perhaps be surprised to learn, gentlemen, that you are in imminent danger of dying at this moment!"

The guns jerked. Coronza's eyes narrowed. Jimmy Christopher's lips thinned more tightly.... His pressure upon the hidden spring in the little golden death's-head now released it. Unseen by the others, a tiny cap—the crown of the skull—flew up. From a cavity inside, a tiny ball rolled into Jimmy Christopher's palm. Deftly he closed the lid, keeping the black pellet in his fingers.

"You will observe," he went on, during the tight silence that followed, "this charm I wear. You may suppose that it is my good-luck piece. It is, I assure you, quite the opposite. I call it, if you will, my bad-luck charm—for an excellent reason!"

The Spaniard snapped: "Take your hands away from it! At once!"

Operator 5 obeyed casually. "For years," he declared, "I have worn this charm—worn it against exactly such an emergency as this. The time would surely come some day, I knew, when it would provide me with the only way out of a serious predicament. The charm, you see, is in reality a case for—this!"

Between his forefinger and thumb, Operator 5 lifted the tiny black sphere. The men around the table stared at it, puzzled, fearful. Jimmy Christopher continued slowly:

"It is a thin shell—so thin that the slightest pressure of my fingers will crush it—so fragile that it will break if dropped only a few inches. It contains a concentration of a substance called *diphenolchlorasine*. I see that some of you recognize the name! It is, as you know, the deadliest poison known to science—a liquid that becomes gas instantly on exposure to air—a gas that kills with the swiftness of lightning. There is enough contained within this pellet to destroy us all before any of you can move."

Jimmy Christopher saw the faces of the men at the table turn white. He continued to hold the pellet of doom lightly between finger and thumb.

"When it bursts I shall, of course, die instantly," he said levelly. "I shall die as quickly as you. I consider that my life is a small price to pay for eliminating the danger which you men constitute to my government. We are, as I have said, gentlemen, facing a show-down."

Coronza snapped: "Put it back! *Madre de Dios*, put it back!"

"Hardly!" Operator 5 smiled slowly.

"Shoot if you wish, gentlemen—the pellet will drop and shatter. If you attempt to take it from me, you will inevitably crush it. Perhaps you prefer me to break it myself. I am tightening my fingers on it now. I regret the necessity, gentlemen, but in a moment—in a moment—"

UNMOVING THE espionage agents stood around the table. Their guns were leveled, but no one of them dared pull the trigger. Their hands were itching to snatch the pellet of doom away, but no one of them dared move. They peered at the tiny black sphere in a fascination of terror as Operator 5's thumb and finger bore upon it....

"I bid you, gentlemen—!"

Blast!

Swift as the stroke of doom, the explosion rocked its power through the house. Suddenly, with all the force of a rending earthquake added to the fury of a lightning bolt, the shock jarred through the walls. One moment, the room had been fearfully hushed; the next, a thunderous concussion ripped through it, bursting window-panes outward, cracking the walls, sagging the floor, shattering the ceiling, gusting flame and unbreathable fumes into the air. The ripping, rending power, crashed through the room like a knell presaging cosmic eternity.

Operator 5 leaped back as the room became transformed into a splintering mass of destruction. Swiftly he rolled the black pellet into his palm and closed his hand tightly around it—tightly, yet gently, around the fragile shell imprisoning the deadly gas. Ripping fury raged around him, deafening, blinding, staggering. At the first terrific jar, the light blinked out and the flickering glare of fire glinted through the shattered windows. Walls, ceiling, floor, were torn by a holocaust that rained wreckage through the air.

Behind Jimmy Christopher, a wall buckled. He leaped forward, throwing himself beneath the stout table. Choking dust enveloped him; ear-rending crashes followed swiftly, rocking the house like a thing of cardboard. Shrieks of pain pierced the rumbling echoes of the concussion—moans and cries of anguish became a chorus of terror. Above Operator 5, the table splintered, and a heavy beam plunged through, driving into the broken floor beside his body. He lay breathless amid whipping destruction as a second earth-rending shock shook the world.

In that chaos, there was no time, no day, no night—only the storming of savage, eternal forces. Stunned, Jimmy Christopher huddled beneath his shelter while the shaking rumble of the explosions beat away like a subsiding surf. All around and above him, the house trembled and crackled as he began to crawl from beneath the table. He paused, blinded by flying dust, and through sense of touch alone found the golden death-charm and pressed the spring that released the cap. Gingerly, he replaced the pellet of death within the hollow and imprisoned it there. As he groped to free himself of fallen timbers, he heard the snarl of a motor, the crackling of wood outside the house, and a rush of power in the street.

He struggled to his feet, fighting against a jungle of wreckage which he could scarcely see through rolling clouds of dust. In the fog, red light flared—a glare carrying in through the windows, warning of a roaring blaze beyond the house. Operator 5 groped frantically to the rear of the room, and saw a door wrenched open—the door beside which Jaime Coronza had been standing. He shouldered through it, twisted to a broken window, peered out upon a blaze that dimmed the sun.

Where the oil refinery had stood, great clouds of fire, white-hearted, black-skinned with the soot of burning oil, were rolling skyward. Tremendous tanks had burst under the impact of the explosion. The fence had vanished in splinters. The earth was gashed deep with the forces of the concussion. A howling wind tore through the air, stirred by the explosion, while the great inferno raged.

CURRENTS OF air sucked dust from the shattered windows as Operator 5 turned back. He struggled again into the room where the espionage agents had met—where chaos had struck. In the thinning mist, he saw men lying on the broken, debris-piled floor. He fought to the first—Okato Hinzu, lying with chest crushed by a fallen timber, dead. He turned to a second— the German ex-Intelligence agent, who lay with broken head. Jimmy Christopher struggled to the corner where Seaton Glave lay lifeless. Again he turned, hearing a mumble of agony and saw, pinned beneath a mass of wreckage, the man who had turned traitor to the United States Intelligence—R-9.

R-9 was moaning; his face was twisting with excruciating pain. He stared, clutched at Operator 5. "Oh, God—God! I—I sold out to Coronza! If he's not dead—watch him! Warn the President! Warn—oh, God!"

R-9's head lolled as unconsciousness overcame him. Jimmy Christopher turned away grimly. He worked back to Slobel

163

while the light of the flames played into the room. He thrust hands into the pockets of the German's coat. He straightened, gripping several thin, tubular objects. He searched farther, found nothing, and struggled to the spot where Okato Hinzu lay. Reaching inside Hinzu's coat, he felt a crackle of paper and jerked an envelope into the flickering flare.

He peered at it only long enough to realize that it was a message in cipher. He thrust it into his pocket also, groped again to the burst door at the rear. He pushed fallen timbers aside, shouldered through another door while nails dug through his clothing and bit into his flesh. He staggered into the open at the rear of the house, stared around. A whole block of homes had become a mass of wreckage—their roofs destroyed, their walls burst, their windows shattered. The garage behind the house where the spies had met was leaning askew—its doors were broken down, exposing an empty stall. Someone had forced the car out; someone had managed to escape the house and flee.

Desperately, Operator 5 leaped across scattered fragments of wood toward the street. In the air, through the rumbling of the flames, the scream of sirens was sounding. As he went in a stumbling run down the street, he glimpsed red fire-engines streaking toward the burning refinery. He paused beside the Intelligence car and ducked in. Its top was splintered by flying fragments. Jimmy Christopher snapped on the current of the wireless transmitter, scarcely breathed until the tubes heated, until the hiss of a carrier wave sounded in the 'phones he clamped to his ears.

"Five-Four-One" he blurted into the microphone. "Calling Five-Four-One!"

A voice rang in his ears. "Five-Four-One reporting! Thank God you're safe! I saw the explosion! For God's sake—?"

"That car!" Jimmy Christopher snapped. "Did you see it leave? Did you spot it?"

"Yes! I've got it in the glasses now! It's heading south as fast as it can travel!"

"Follow it! Keep it in sight! Watch it no matter where it goes! Trail it as long as your gas lasts! Keep the reports coming!"

"Right! It seems to be working toward the main highway. It may be heading for Washington!"

Washington! The name chilled Operator 5. In his ears again sounded R-9's breathless, pain-torn voice. "Watch Coronza! Warn the President!" It meant—?

CHAPTER 13
SPY'S ULTIMATUM

O **PERATOR 5** strode swiftly into the secret office of Z-7 in headquarters KT, New York. He had sped without a stop from the west side of the Hudson. As he turned to his desk, the door opened and a man in an acid-stained smock quickly entered the room. He was one of the most expert of the Intelligence chemists; his face was pasty with anxiety.

"Z-7," he declared, "ordered one of the containers brought here and tested. It is filled with pure nitroglycerin! Enough to have—"

"Your analysis of the solvent gas?" Jimmy Christopher snapped. "Are you making headway?"

"None! It defies analysis. We are doing our best, but I'm afraid it is hopeless. We will keep on the job, of course, but—it's the most difficult analysis we've ever tackled and I can promise no results whatever!"

"Keep at it!"

Jimmy Christopher removed from his pocket the communication he had taken from the dead Okato Hinzu. He peered at the message—a series of groups of apparently meaningless letters:

DHJPW BNAKE UHWCK ECGUA TYAQN ZIPIS
WNHYY HHSVI LKPWA BYRCE MNKPU QWPOX….

He drew open a drawer of a cabinet, drew out frequency-tables which he had prepared, ingenious short-cuts to the solution of ciphers which he had devised and tested against the most difficult secret messages. Drawing pad and pencil close, he set feverishly to work. He did not glance up as a man approached his desk—X-2, acting chief of headquarters KT.

"Z-7 is at the hospital with Professor Yerian," the New York chief told Operator 5 quickly. "Yerian's condition is extremely serious. He is delirious. Is it true that he destroyed his data?"

"Yes!" Operator 5's pencil flew as he spoke. "We must depend now on making our defenses as strong as possible with the small oil supply we have. It is only a question of a short time until it will give out, but—"

"Our Atlantic fleet was waiting for a new consignment of oil from the New Jersey refinery that exploded this morning," X-2 declared. "It means that the fleet will scarcely be able to move

166

until a fresh shipment is sent across the country—oil that the Pacific fleet needs as desperately. We are trying to produce oil by the distillation of shale, but the work cannot possibly proceed at a fast enough rate and we can count on scarcely any help from that quarter!"

A shirt-sleeved man from the communications-room entered the office. He snatched away the proffered message; his eyes widened as he read it; then he slapped it on the desk in front of Jimmy Christopher:

... KT-NY THRU WDC-13... WARSHIPS AGAIN REPORTED IN PACIFIC... UNIDENTIFIED FLEET STEAMING TOWARD PANAMA CANAL... OUR FLEET UNABLE TO HEAD ENEMY OFF... LACK OF FUEL HAMPERS OUR MOVEMENT... CANAL ZONE WARNED TO PREPARE FOR ATTACK... W-17 LA....

"God!" X-2 blurted. "The submarine in the Gulf, and this battle fleet approaching from the Pacific! The Canal will be struck from both sides unless we find enough oil to get our ships into position and our planes into the air in sufficient numbers!" OPERATOR 5 gestured. "We're doing everything possible—we can do nothing more. X-2, see that I'm not disturbed except for the most pressing emergency. This code is most import-ant—I've got to get it deciphered."

"Right!"

X-2 strode from the room, closed the door behind him. Again Operator 5 tackled the secret message. He realized at once that it was a transposition, not a substitution type, through his frequency tables. He detected indications at once that the transposition was double. Quietly and quickly he sought to discover the pattern. His years of work in deciphering difficult ciphers helped him now. Suddenly, his pencil began to leap across the pad:

Okato Hinzu—imperative orders—wireless operator aboard submarine Annihilator executed because of suspected treachery—no other man aboard expert enough to handle messages—your services needed desperately—follow these directions—charter airplane and carry parachute flying so that you reach point in Caribbean 14 degrees fifty minutes Latitude 81 degrees Longitude exactly midnight tonight—at light signal, use parachute—Annihilator will pick you up—necessary you take key in order to handle coördinating orders for attack on Canal—Kuttman, Commander.

Jimmy Christopher peered at the translation with darkened eyes. Striding to a file, he removed a folder which contained data on the international spy Hinzu and a photograph. He studied it so intently that he scarcely heard the door fly open and X-2 stride in.

"Operator 5! A code message from Paris! God! It means greater danger than we imagined!"

Jimmy Christopher read the translated cable dispatch rapidly—and his face lost color:

... KT-NY BY CABLE THROUGH WDC-13... DETAILS OF NEW WEAPON JUST UNCOV-

ERED HERE... SUBMARINE SECRETLY BUILT
FINANCED BY POLITICAL FACTIONS COMBINED
IN NEW DANGEROUS ALLIANCE CALLED
GREAT ENTENTE... SUBMARINE ANNIHILATOR
CONVERTIBLE TO ARMED TANK... ARMED WITH
HEAVY GUNS AND TORPEDOES... CANNOT BE
HARMED BY AERIAL BOMBS... HEAVIER AND
MORE POWERFUL THAN LAND TANKS... CAN
RETREAT TO WATER... INTERCEPTED MESSAGE
REVEALS IT WILL ATTACK PANAMA CANAL TO
DESTROY LOCKS TO BARRICADE WATERWAY...
EXACT DETAILS UNKNOWN... MOST DESTRUC-
TIVE MOBILE WEAPON IN WORLD... ONLY HEAVY
ARTILLERY CAN STOP IT... WARN ZONE GUARDS
AND COAST DEFENSE BATTERIES.. ATTACK AT
ANY MOMENT... G-9 PF....

Jimmy Christopher sprang to his feet. His glance flashed back
to the secret message he had deciphered. He turned with his eyes
glinting darkly to X-2—but the shrill ring of the telephone bell
brought him to a pause. He jerked up the instrument.

"Operator 5!" rang over the wire. "Z-7 calling! I am talking
from the hospital. Yerian has regained consciousness fully. He
is asking for you. Can you come?"

"Chief, I have just uncovered information of the greatest
importance! I am ordering an airplane made ready now at
Mitchell Field. I have to get to Washington. I must lay this
information before the President without delay. Every moment
is precious! The President must order full mobilization if we are

to meet this new threat! Reach me by wireless in case of emergency!"

Operator 5 clashed the receiver on its hook, spun to face the pallid X-2 "Order the fastest plane at Mitchell Field to be made ready for me at once!"

ABOVE BOLLING FIELD, Washington, D.C., the swift army combat crate leaned into a circle. Its pilot had sent it flashing through the sky at top speed on orders from Operator 5. In the rear cubby, Jimmy Christopher, 'phones fitted to his ears and a spider microphone before his lips, watched the ground spin. The plane was spiraling for a landing when a rushing sound stirred the receivers and a far-away voice spoke.

"Five-Four-One calling! Five-Four-One calling! Report for Operator 5: We have followed the automobile as far as possible. We have run out of fuel and are being forced to land. The car has already gone ahead, out of sight. We are north of Baltimore. It's certain that the car is heading for Washington."

Again Operator 5 felt dread weight in his heart as he remembered R-9's dying warning. "Warn the President!" Jimmy Christopher grimly removed the 'phones and mike as his plane drove down to the smooth tarmac of Bolling Field. His lids lowered with thought.

Immediately the combat ship braked, he slipped out of the pit. His radioed orders, flashing ahead, had brought an Intelligence car to the field. He hurried to it. As he dropped into the rear seat, he ordered the driver with a snap: "The White House!"

The car sped into the heart of Washington—through streets weirdly quiet and empty. The capital of the nation was as stricken

170

by the oil shortage as every other great city. A pall of paralysis hung over it, a hush of fear. The Intelligence car turned into Pennsylvania Avenue while Operator 5 sat tensely, burning with impatience to reach his destination.

He had snapped the switch of the radio. An announcer's voice began to speak, following the clang of a bell, as the car approached the White House and slowed. The words vibrated with excitement:

"War is being advocated in Congress! One of the most startling speeches in the history of the nation is to be made on the floor of the Senate now by Senator Dreer of New York. We have made arrangements to broadcast his words. Senator Dreer is speaking, ladies and gentlemen!"

There followed a resonant voice that could be heard echoing from the walls of the great Senate Chamber at the hub of the capitol.

"Gentlemen, we face attack! We face extinction! We confront an emergency that will wipe us out of existence unless we act! We need oil. Gentlemen, we must get oil! We must use our dwindling reserves to obtain more oil at all costs! Our navy, our army, our air forces, are powerful enough at this moment to save us, but it is only a matter of hours until our defenses will be crippled and we will lie supine and helpless before any invader. Let us invade before we are invaded! Let us attack before we are attacked! Let us send our armed forces across our borders with one order paramount: 'Get oil! Get oil, for without oil we will perish!' I advocate an act of war, gentlemen. I plead that if we must be destroyed, let us go down fighting!"

A roar of approval sounded from the radio—voices raised in desperate fervor.

Gravely, Operator 5 clicked off the radio as the Intelligence car passed through the gate of the White House. Secret Service men were on duty near the doors. Jimmy Christopher passed through the entrance to meet the President's Secretary. The worried, middle-aged man declared nervously: "The President is waiting for you in his study, sir."

OPERATOR 5 entered the room from which startling proclamations had been issued in a desperate national effort to conserve oil. Behind an imposing desk, a strong-faced man came to his feet and extended a steady hand to Jimmy Christopher. His manner was kindly though tense; the pressure of his fingers was firm and warm, and his eyes were keenly alert.

"I have come to you on a matter of the utmost importance, Mr. President," Operator 5 declared.

He placed on the President's desk the secret message he had deciphered, and a copy of the Paris dispatch informing the United States Intelligence of the submarine-tank. The Chief Executive read them rapidly and his eyes rose to Operator 5's.

"Mr. President!" Operator 5 spoke in a firm, level tone. "The import of this secret message is that the submarine-tank, the *Annihilator*, is the mobile headquarters of the attacking forces. From that engine, war orders will go out directing the blows to be struck at the Panamá Canal and the invasion planned to follow. This message opens an opportunity to combat the planned attack secretly. I have evolved a plan whereby—"

A knock sounded on the door of the study, interrupting

Jimmy Christopher. At the President's call, it opened. The President's secretary strode into the room, blinking with dismay, groping for words to convey his message. He exclaimed:

"There is a man at the gate, sir, insisting upon seeing you. He declares that once you know his name, you will admit him immediately. He states that he is bringing a message of vital importance."

"His name?" the President inquired.

"Coronza, sir! Señor Jaime Coronza!"

Operator 5 jerked to his feet. The glitter in his eyes grew brighter as he peered at the Chief Executive. Color had drained from the President's face at the sound of the name.

"Coronza? Here?"

Jimmy Christopher spoke crisply: "Mr. President, this is a daring move of Coronza's—and it is highly necessary for us to learn his purpose. I suggest that you admit him."

The President looked startled. "You will remain here with me, of course?"

"Yes!" To the secretary, Jimmy Christopher ordered: "Tell Coronza he may come in. Treat him like a privileged visitor. Bring him directly to this study."

OUTSIDE THE study door, a voice sounded, that of the secretary. "Step in, sir." The knob turned; the door opened. Into the room strode the lean, square-shouldered espionage agent, Coronza.

Jaime Coronza's gaze turned to Operator 5's face, and he smiled. He strode toward the desk, bowed with an elaborate show of respect. Jimmy Christopher's sharp gaze searched the espionage agent's face as Coronza spoke:

"Señor President. I should not request the privilege of seeing you unless my business were of the greatest importance. You are aware, I know, of my—profession. You know that I, more than any other man, am responsible for placing the United States in this sorry situation. I wish to assure you that I mean you no harm personally, that I am completely unarmed, and that I will need only a few minutes of your time."

The President nodded shortly. "You are, Señor Coronza, the most distinguished—in fact, the only—member of your profession who has ever paid me a call. You realize, I'm sure, that you are being watched and that you are under arrest. Immediately after you finish your business, you will be imprisoned and—"

"Ah, no!" Coronza interrupted with a suave gesture. "I do not consider myself under arrest, Señor President, and I do not fancy that I will be made prisoner. Once you learn the nature of my mission."

"What is it?"

Coronza bowed again, while Operator 5 regarded him alertly. "I came here, Señor President—to put it as briefly as possible—to have you order the United States Intelligence Service disbanded immediately."

The President stared at the amazing coolness of Coronza; he tightened at the unutterable insolence. The espionage agent smiled again.

"I will explain," he said easily. "The United States Intelligence Service is, I confess, the most dangerous organization with which the coming new government, which will take the place of the United States, might cope. In order to remove that danger, your Intelligence organization must be destroyed. It must, to be precise, cease to function altogether within twenty-four hours!"

"You cannot believe, Señor Coronza," the President said firmly, "that your suggestion will be followed?"

"Ah, yes, Señor President! Allow me to explain further. It is my secret organization, as you know, which is responsible for the sabotage of your few producing oil-wells and your principal refineries. We have worked with precision. Our only error was the premature explosion of the New Jersey refinery this morning—a stupid blunder which cannot occur again. It is quite true that every oil-well which is now producing in the United States has been mined by my men. At my signal any or all of them will be destroyed. I have only to speak and the last drop of petroleum will cease flowing within this country. I assure you solemnly, Señor President, that this is absolutely true!"

The President's face darkened. "I cannot accept that statement as the truth!"

CORONZA SHRUGGED. "There were," he said, "not long ago, over three-hundred-thousand oil wells in the United States, most of them producing. There are now only a few hundred supplying oil. It has not been difficult for us to make our arrangements. Each of these producing wells is mined. A mere movement of a finger by one of my agents miles away will be sufficient to destroy any or all of them. It is this fact, Señor President, which leads me to believe that you will follow my suggestion to disorganize the United States Intelligence Service at once."

"Unless I do so, you mean to say," The Chief Executive answered, "you will order the nation's wells destroyed?"

"Exactly, Señor President!" He drew a folded paper from his pocket. He spread it on the corner of the desk and disclosed it to be a map of the United States, marked with red squares.

"This chart shows the location of the few remaining fields producing oil. At my signal every one of them will be destroyed!"

"I cannot believe it!" the President gasped. He struggled to control his emotion. "I still see no reason why you cannot be arrested here and now—why this damnable plot need go a step further."

"Ah, Señor!" the cool Spaniard breathed. "If I do not communicate with my men at a certain time—if my mission here is not successful—the wells will be destroyed anyway!"

"It's a bluff!" the President grated. "It's a display of colossal impudence, Mr. Coronza. I do not believe you!"

Jaime Coronza smiled amiably, glanced at his wrist watch. "I can prove to you that it is not. In exactly one minute, unless I alter my orders, the Ozoro field in the Fort Texas field will be a thing of the past."

The Chief Executive glanced haggardly at Operator 5, a question in his eyes.

"I think perhaps Mr. Coronza might be released," Operator 5 said. "He is shrewd enough—"

"I cannot!" the President exclaimed. "My duty—"

"Ah, *Señors!*" Coronza smiled. "Do not fret. In a moment, everything will be quite clear—quite proven."

Again the President raised puzzled eyes to Jimmy Christopher. It was plain to see that the Chief Executive was faced with one of the most serious decisions of his career.

Coronza smiled evilly and said nothing. The President peered at him uncertainly. Operator 5 noted the confident gleam in the spy's eyes. Silence continued in the President's study; long, tense moments passed. Each second tightened Jimmy Christopher's nerves. He rose swiftly—the President jerked—yet Coronza did not stir—when the telephone jangled.

The Chief Executive raised the instrument. "Yes!" Then "Yes, here! The message?" Again, huskily, "Yes!" He returned the instrument to peer at Operator 5 gauntly.

"The Ozoro well in the East Texas Field was destroyed by an explosion a few moments ago!"

Coronza rose. "There is your proof, Señor President. You will find it impossible to alter the situation. Therefore I repeat my suggestion. You are to issue orders that the United States Intelligence Service be disbanded within twenty-four hours. If you do not do this, the wells now producing oil in this country will be destroyed, one after another, until they are all gone. Within the space of a few hours, every one will be burning!"

CORONZA, WHILE the President stared and Operator 5 listened in cold fury, drew another paper from his pocket.

"This is a list," he declared, "of every agent in the United States Intelligence. Operator 5 knows, I am sure, how I obtained it. This is, of course, only a copy. I presume, Señor President, to give orders to you now, not suggestions. These men, these secret agents, every one, must be transported to the Federal Penitentiaries and made prisoners—including this young man known as Operator 5. All over the country, your agents must be incarcerated. We have this complete list—we will check it thoroughly. Every operator must be made a prisoner within twenty-four hours, Señor President, or, at noon tomorrow, the wells of this country will begin to blaze!"

The President went pale. "It's impossible! You're under arrest, Coronza! You will never have an opportunity to give your signal!"

Coronza shrugged. "Does the Señor President forget that my men are waiting for me now? As I warned you unless I come to that place within—" Coronza glanced at his wristwatch again—"thirty minutes, my absence will in itself act as a signal. Your oil-wells will begin to explode even sooner! You may throw me into prison if you wish—but it will mean the sacrifice of the last drop of petroleum in the United States!"

The Chief Executive stood speechless. Coronza's evil smile grew.

"You are still doubtful? You doubt that this destruction will begin if I do not return to my men at once? Then detain me! You wish to save your oil, to retain your last fighting power? Then allow me to depart, and within twenty-four hours, order every Intelligence man imprisoned and the organization destroyed once and for all!"

Operator 5 stepped forward grimly. Quietly he said: "Coronza, we have heard quite enough. I have not the slightest doubt that you have spoken the truth. You will welcome an opportunity to sound your signal to destroy our last wells. You are the most dangerous espionage agent living, and you have proved it."

Coronza bowed. "Then—?"

"You may go!"

Again, a suave bow. *"Gracias, Señors. Adios!"* The spy turned and strode with a swagger to the study door. Operator 5 followed him through it, and his command brought the Chief of the White House detail into the corridor. "Señor Coronza is to be allowed a safe departure!" Coronza, his evil smile spreading, strode straight toward the historic entrance of the White House.

Operator 5 turned back to the President's study as the telephone bell shrilled. The Chief Executive was staring at him white-faced, ignoring the bell. Jimmy Christopher exclaimed:

"Mr. President, it is impossible not to concede to Coronza's demands at this moment. We must, at any cost, save our last reserve of oil from the destruction he threatens. If necessary, by noon tomorrow, we must disband the Intelligence. I hope that, before that time, we shall be able to strike a blow which will render Coronza's ring and the waiting attackers powerless."

The Chief Executive sank into his chair. "I can see no way out! It will be impossible for us to discover Coronza's mines— hundreds of them!—by noon tomorrow. We would need the entire army to police those oil-fields, the thousands of miles of pipelines. And to scatter the army now to make the effort would be fatal—it would leave us vulnerable to any invasion! There is no move we can possibly make!"

"One, Mr. President!" Operator 5 declared. "One last move! It is a desperate risk—for if it fails, nothing can save us. I have a plan that must be put into execution at once if even that gamble is to be played."

The President reached quickly for the telephone while Operator 5 answered briskly:

"I will inform you of my move immediately. I will map out the last details! Until then—new warnings to all our defenses to be prepared against attack!"

The Chief Executive spoke quickly into the instrument, then offered it to Jimmy Christopher. "For you, Operator 5. Z-7 talking from New York!"

Jimmy Christopher spoke crisply into the transmitter: "Chief!"

"I am calling to urge you again to come to Professor Yerian. He is sinking fast, but he is still asking for you—pleading to see you. Acting on his instructions, his daughter locked herself in his hospital room with him, and he will admit no one until you come. We cannot ignore his request when—"

"I will return to New York immediately, Chief!" Operator 5 answered with instant decision. "In the meantime, order one of the fastest planes available to be made ready for me there. It cannot be an army crate—it must be commercial. It is to be fuelled for a non-stop flight beyond our southern border. Important, Chief—and I'm coming now!"

CHAPTER 14
THE *ANNIHILATOR* WAITS

DOWN THE gleaming white hospital corridor Jimmy Christopher strode with Z-7 at his side. He had flashed over the air-lane from Washington. A swift car, awaiting him, had carried him to the building. Now he paused, the Washington chief at his side, at the door of the room in which the Professor Yerian lay dying.

He knocked. Through the panels, a girl's voice sounded: "No one can come in!"

"I am Operator 5."

A pause followed. Doré Yerian's voice exclaimed, inside the room, "Father—he's come!" The scientist's husky tones answered: "Let him in—quickly! Let him in!" A key turned in the lock; the door opened. Doré Yerian peered at Jimmy Christopher with anxiety clouding her eyes, her face white, and stood aside.

Operator 5 quietly entered the room. On the bed, propped on pillows, Professor Yerian lay. His face was white as the spotless sheets; his eyes were burning with a feverish light. He attempted to rise as Jimmy Christopher entered, but sank back with a moan of pain. His hand fluttered, seized Operator 5's. He gasped: "Come close! Listen to what I have to say! I cannot last long now! Listen!"

His lips trembled; his voice was a husky whisper. Operator 5 leaned close to hear.

"Doré—Doré has told me. You—you saved her from being

181

killed—by that damnable fiend who shot me. He would have killed her, if you had not—stopped him. I am grateful—grateful!"

Operator 5 answered quietly: "I could do nothing else. I only regret that I could not stop Coronza before—"

"No! My life does not matter! It is lived—I have finished my work. Nothing means anything to me now but Doré—nothing! Keep her safe! See that she is not harmed! She must not be drawn into this merciless fight for oil. It will be my fault if—if she suffers because others think she knows my secret. There is only—only one way to stop that—only one way I can repay you for saving her."

"I expect no—"

"Listen!" Professor Yerian's hand groped frantically toward his pillows. It slipped beneath them and removed a sheaf of papers. They were scribbled closely with figures, with chemical symbols, with close, precise writing. Yerian thrust them toward Operator 5.

"Take these! I would—I would give them to no one else in the world. They are yours—yours personally, to do with as you wish. I am putting into your hands a wealth greater than that of any man who ever lived—power greater than ever existed before. It is yours—all yours—in return for your promise to keep Doré safe from the merciless battle for oil!"

"You have my promise. Professor Yerian. I swear no harm will come to her. You must—"

"That is the data of the Yerian process! I have redrawn it from memory. I spoke the truth when I said—only one written copy existed—and I destroyed that. But every figure—every detail—was stamped on my mind—by years of work. That man—knew it. That's why—he tried to kill me. It is all here—the formula for the solvent gas—the pressure factors—everything! Yours!" OPERATOR 5 sat chilled, his fingers fastened upon the precious sheets. Yerian clawed at the first of them and in one trembling hand lifted a pencil. He leaned to write below a few lines already scrawled on the page. Operator 5 read them as his pencil moved:

> To the young man known as James Christopher I transfer and bequeath all rights of whatever nature, exclusively and for all time, in the Yerian Process of oil-well revivification.

Professor Yerian painfully signed his name. He pushed the inscribed sheet to Jimmy Christopher. He dropped the pencil, extended his trembling hand.

"Thank you, my boy! You have made me happy—you have restored my faith in man—to know that Doré—"

Suddenly Professor Yerian went limp. Suddenly he sagged into the pillows, his eyes closed, his head lolling. A stifled cry broke from Doré Yerian. She started toward the bed and stopped, paralyzed with grief. Operator 5 lowered the scientist's hand and rose, dark lines etching the skin around his eyes. He turned quietly, and left the room, and closed the door.

"He died—with his daughter's name on his lips."

Z-7 was staring. "But he reproduced the data? He—"

Operator 5 nodded gravely, strode quickly across the corridor and thrust into another room. It was occupied by no patient. He carried the precious document to the desk, dipped a pen, and rapidly wrote. He turned, and handed the data sheets to Z-7. The Washington chief peered at the lines Jimmy Christopher had written:

> To the Government of the United States I herewith deliver all rights to the Yerian Process granted me by Professor Norton Yerian.
>
> James Christopher.

Z-7's eyes glittered with a deep fire. "You need not do this. You can receive royalties on every barrel of oil produced by the Yerian method! You will become the richest and most powerful man in the world if you make that stipulation!"

"The Yerian Process," Operator 5 declared levelly, "is now the property of the United States Government without a single reservation."

Z-7 stared. "This means," he said, "that every well in the United States will immediately begin flowing again—that we will possess a strength greater that any other nation on the face of globe!"

"Chief!" Jimmy Christopher cried: "Order our labs to begin making the solvent gas at once, in as great quantity as possible! Rush crews to the abandoned oil fields. Order any necessary pumps and apparatus manufactured. Not a moment must be spared, Chief, to get oil flowing through the arteries of the nation. Not a moment!"

A SWIFT Intelligence car brought Z-7 to the door of Address Y—the home of John Christopher. Tim Donovan admitted him.

The wide-eyed boy bounded after the Washington chief, up the stairs and into the living-room. Z-7 paused, facing Ex-Operator Q-6 and Diane Elliot, and asked breathlessly: "Operator 5—is he here?"

"He came a few moments ago, Chief," John Christopher answered. "He went into his workshop and bolted the door. I don't know what he's doing, but—"

Z-7 smacked his fist into palm. "The President has just issued his proclamation ordering all producing oil-wells shut down—a move to circumvent Coronza's threat. Let that damned spy blow up those wells now! Our labs are rushing the manufacture of Yerian's solvent gas. We're speeding supplies, machinery and crews to fields formerly abandoned. Within a few hours, vast quantities of petroleum will be flowing from wells that we've believed exhausted!"

"Then we're assured of an adequate supply, Chief?"

"Fully adequate—a supply great enough to last us two thousand years! Our problem at this moment is time. We're doing our utmost to get the Yerian process into use at the soonest possible moment. Oil will be rushed by air from the fields, to our naval ships, to protected refineries, the moment it begins to flow. Now, by God, we can fight!"

A rattle of a knob drew their attention to the door at the rear—the entrance to Operator 5's workshop. It opened quickly. A startled gasp broke from the lips of Z-7 as he peered at the figure who strode through. Diane Elliot gazed in amazement; Tim Donovan's eyes widened.

The man they looked upon was saffron-skinned and slant-

He drifted down to the sleek back of the *Annihilator!*

eyed; his face was masked with the inscrutability of the Oriental; it had a sinister, evil aspect. He paused, and, slowly, smiled. Z-7, still peering at him, exclaimed: "Okato Hinzu!"

The voice that answered was high-pitched; the words were clipped. "Okato Hinzu is dead!" And immediately the tones changed to a familiar crispness. "Okay, Chief! I'll chance it!"

"Jimmy!" Tim Donovan blurted. "Gee, Jimmy! I didn't even recognize you!"

Operator 5 strode swiftly into the room. "I've done my best to duplicate Hinzu's appearance," he declared. "It's the first step of my plan. We've no time to waste, Chief! Is the plane I asked for waiting?"

"Yes! But what do you intend to do?"

"I'm going to follow the orders received from the submarine-tank by Hinzu, Chief. Perhaps my disguise won't pass, but I've got to take that chance. I'm going to get on that sub and act as wireless operator for it. It will place me in a powerful position."

"And in a mighty dangerous one!" Z-7 protested. "If you're discovered!"

"It's our only chance, Chief! Orders are to go out from that sub to the other units of attack—the camouflaged fleet in the Pacific, for instance. If I can alter those orders before I send them, I can disrupt the plan. If I can flash you by wireless and inform you of the sub tactics, our defenses may be able to destroy it. There's no other way we can save the Canal or stop the invasion from the South."

Z-7 PRESSED the accelerator hard to the floor-boards and his eyes smoldered as the sedan streaked.

"Once I'm off, Chief," Operator 5 continued, "I want you to return to Washington with Tim. Put Tim at one of the short-wave receiver units. He and I have trained ourselves in a certain cipher, and we're able to send and receive messages in it and translate them automatically, although the cipher is completely baffling to anyone intercepting the message. Tim's service is necessary in order to save as much time as possible—the difference between defeat and victory.

"Tim, whatever message I send is to be obeyed to the exact letter. Everything will depend on that—the fate of the whole nation. Absolutely nothing must interfere—nothing, you understand?"

"I'll do it, Jimmy!"

Z-7 swerved the car off the road, through the gate of Roosevelt Field. He stopped the car at the inner fence, beside the white buildings, and hurried down the row of hangars with Operator 5 at his side. They came to a powerful cabin monoplane which was waiting, its prop idling. The pilot stationed beside it saluted.

"Ready?" Jimmy Christopher asked.

"Yes, sir!"

"We'll take off at once!"

He turned. The four gazed at him anxiously, strangely—for the perfection of his disguise still deceived them, masked the Jimmy Christopher they knew. Yet the voice, speaking quietly, was that of Operator 5.

"So long, Dad! Di, you've helped me wonderfully. Tim, you'll hop off for Washington with Z-7 now and camp at that short-wave receiver. There's nothing more anyone of you can do—the rest of it is entirely up to me."

"Jimmy!" Diane exclaimed. "Can't I—can't I come with you?"

Not this time, Di. It's impossible." Operator 5's artificially slanted eyes darkened. "You've been great—all of you. There's—there's a chance that I won't come back. If I don't—good luck!"

John Christopher's hand gripped Operator 5's tightly. Tim Donovan stared wide-eyed; impulsively he flung his arms around Jimmy Christopher and choked back a sob. Diane Elliot seized his hand; suddenly, she pressed her trembling, red lips to his. He turned away tensely, Z-7 shaking his hand.

"You've got to come back, Jimmy Christopher!" broke from Diane Elliot's lips. "You've got to come back!"

IN WASHINGTON, D.C., secret Intelligence headquarters WDC-13, nerve-center of the United States undercover system, lay hidden behind the grimy front of a cheap restaurant. In one of the windowless rooms there was silence. Its walls were paneled with short-wave wireless apparatus. In it, while a hushed night lay over the nation—while terror trembled the hearts of millions and invasion threatened—four persons, besides the radio experts, waited.

Tim Donovan perched before a receiver with 'phones clamped to his ears. The rush of a carrier wave was sounding—the transmitted power of the unit in the plane carrying Operator 5 southward through the night. Behind him stood Z-7, Ex-Operator Q-6 and Diane Elliot. From Jimmy Christopher's plane messages had flashed and now they were tensely waiting for another.

On the wall, an electric clock indicated the hour—and the red second hand was spinning toward the instant of midnight.

Tim Donovan jerked as a voice carried through the ether from far away—the voice of Jimmy Christopher.

"Calling WDC-13! Operator 5 calling! We have reached our destination. We are circling now above the designated point. We made it by a margin of seconds. I am waiting now for the light signal!"

The second hand of his watch ticked to the dot of midnight and a light flashed below!

It stabbed out of the Stygian gloom, a spot far beneath the plane, a beam slashing through the sky. It cut upward in a wide swing. It beat into Operator 5's gleaming eyes as he turned to speak ringingly into the microphone.

"The signal is flashing! Stand by, Tim! Wait for further messages in the special cipher! Going down!"

Quickly he checked the buckles of the parachute harness he had strapped around his body. He signaled the pilot. The plane swung lower, spiraling—swung to a position directly *above* the one gleam of light in all that vast cosmos of darkness. The lessened speed decreased the wind-pressure on the door, and Operator 5 thrust it wider. He poised on the sill, peering down, and—leaped!

He plummeted through pitch blackness; the plane vanished above him. A jerk on the rip-cord brought the pilot-'chute flicking out. Its drag pulled the great silken bell from the pack.

It hummed as it filled and Jimmy Christopher swung in the shroud-lines. Peering down, he gripped the lines, spilled air from the 'chute to direct himself toward the spot of light below. He drifted down toward it—closer through the blackness of space.

The gleam of the searchlight brought an outline out of the darkness of the sea. On the swells, a great bulk was floating. The sleek back of a giant submarine glistened wetly. On its deck men were moving—men in strange uniform. A hatch yawned open. The image grew magnified as Operator 5 dropped. Among the figures on the superstructure he noted one that was huge, commanding. The man in resplendent uniform was peering up at the parachute shining in the light.

AGAIN OPERATOR 5 spilled air from the chute to send him directly to the deck of the sub. His breath came hotly and his fingers tore the buckles of the harness loose as his feet struck. Dragging to the rail, he gripped it as the great bell tore away and went flaccid on the sea. His nerves burned; his eyes gleamed alertly as he executed a brisk about-face and came to attention facing the commanding figure. He spoke in clipped, high-pitched syllables.

"Okato Hinzu reporting for orders, Commander!"

The huge man—Commander Kuttman of the submarine-tank *Annihilator*—twisted his thick, heavy lips into a smile. He peered into Operator 5's disguised face intently. He advanced, offered a hand.

"You have done well, Comrade Hinzu!" he exclaimed in a heavy voice. "It is long since I last saw you in Geneva, when we first evolved the plan which we are now putting into operation.

Let us lose no time. Minutes are precious. Your post is waiting below."

Operator 5 glanced around swiftly. He noted, beneath the wash of the waves at both sides of the sub, great tractor treads— the mechanisms by which the diabolical war engine could leave the water like a turtle and crawl upon land. He noted, fore and aft watertight hatches which must conceal the powerful land-guns of the craft. Smaller cannon were mounted on the superstructure and ready for instant use. He moved behind Commander Kuttman to the open hatch.

When he descended the ladder, into the gleaming space of the sub, he marveled. Being familiar with the mechanism and operation of ordinary underwater vessels, he realized immediately that the *Annihilator* was equipped with protective devices, with attacking weapons, far in advance of any other submarine ever built. It was literally a mobile fort equally at home in water or on land. Around the shining machinery, near the breeches of the concealed cannon, the efficient crew was standing at attention.

Commander Kuttman led Jimmy Christopher aft, into a small steel-walled compartment. On a metal table, sensitive wireless equipment sat. The Commander gestured toward it proudly.

"Your post, Comrade Hinzu. You may take time now to familiarize yourself with the apparatus. There will be important messages shortly. In the meantime, we wait for another distinguished passenger who will accompany us when we disable the Panamá Canal and make the first drive of our invasion."

Operator 5 stood cold as Commander Kuttman strode from the wireless room. Quickly he inspected the installation. It was, he saw at once, of advanced design and extremely powerful. He snapped on the current at once and took the key. Swiftly, trimming the oscillator to the wave-length over which WDC-13 was listening, he tapped out a brief message:

Safely aboard *Annihilator*. Wait!

In Washington, he knew, Tim Donovan was translating that message automatically and relaying it to Z-7.

Jimmy Christopher listened tensely while the giant submarine-tank rode the waves. The Commander had again climbed to the deck; the crew was still waiting. Long minutes passed while Operator 5 surveyed his surroundings. Now, he realized, everything depended upon his disguise. If he were discovered within this war-machine there would be no hope of escape. Falsifying of messages to other attacking units of the Great Entente would involve a grave risk; sending dispatches to WDC-13 would mean an even greater danger. While he waited, cold and anxious, the *Annihilator* swayed in the swells.

SLOWLY A pulsing came into the air, a sound that reached down through the open hatch. It was the droning of an airplane. Operator 5 strode from the wireless room and peered up into the sky. The shaft of the searchlight was again swinging. The light glittered off the wings of a craft soaring far overhead. And as Jimmy Christopher watched, he saw a figure climb overside and jump.

In the white beam, a parachute blossomed. It floated downward while its passenger navigated toward the floating tank-sub. Operator 5 watched with apprehension as the swinging figure magnified in his vision. Ringing steps sounded above when the 'chute passed out of sight. The collapsing bell whisked over the hatch and the voice of Commander Kuttman carried down.

"We are honored! Come below at once, comrade, and we will proceed with the attacking orders!"

Operator 5 stood back as the man who had parachuted to the sub began to descend the ladder. His slanted eyes darkened as he recognized the tall figure, the square shoulders. At the base of the ladder, the new-comer turned—to face Jimmy Christopher.

Operator 5 gazed into the swarthy face, the gleaming eyes of Jaime Coronza.

"Hinzu!" Coronza exclaimed. "I was afraid you were killed in the explosion! *Por Dios,* I did not expect to see you!"

In the high, cracking voice Jimmy Christopher answered: "I am glad to say that I was only slightly hurt, Comrade Coronza! I managed to slip away. I am honored to transmit the orders of Commander Kuttman!"

His heart was cold with a fear that the keen-eyed Coronza was penetrating his disguise; but the Spaniard smiled broadly. "Good! Now there is no time to lose! We are ready! We have the United States in a trap from which it cannot escape!"

"The credit is yours, Comrade Coronza!" Operator 5 declared, hiding the bitterness he felt.

"The United States will be helpless to repulse our attack once it begins. Their oil will give out almost at once! Their Intelligence will be disbanded within twelve hours now through fear of losing their last drop of oil. I tell you, we have worked well! We have made ourselves the greatest power in the world!"

Operator 5, his heart weighted with dread, turned briskly to the wireless room. He flung off coat and hat, sat at the key, and held himself ready. Presently Commander Kuttman marched to the door, and Jaime Coronza appeared behind him.

"Comrade Hinzu, our orders must now be transmitted. Our Pacific fleet is waiting for them. A second fleet is now steaming across the Atlantic, coming into position to bombard New York. Again, a second Pacific fleet is making ready to shell the West Coast cities. Most important is our move to disable the Panamá Canal, which we will accomplish aided by the first Pacific fleet. Here, comrade, are explicit orders to transmit to Commander Jorako."

Kuttman passed the closely written sheet to Operator 5. It was in cipher—disguised so that he could not read its words— but he realized it was an order directing the exact time of the attack calculated to hit the Panamá Canal at its southern outlet. He turned to the key immediately, again trimming the oscillator, and his supple fingers played the key.

While his heart throbbed with apprehension, he flashed into the ether—not the words of the cipher message—but a meaningless jumble of letters!

He paused, returned the message to Commander Kuttman, and searched Coronza's eyes. Had the espionage agent read the senseless dots and dashes sent out? Had he learned that "Hinzu" had not actually transmitted the orders? Jimmy Christopher, breath locked in his lungs, saw Commander Kuttman nod.

"The orders are sent!" he declared.

"Good!"

"Por Dios, we strike!"

KUTTMAN'S EYES were gleaming. "Yes! We are proceeding now at full speed toward Limón Bay. We will leave the water close to the edge of the West Breakwater! Our cannon will be ready immediately when we climb upon land. Our calculations are checked and our first shells are certain to destroy the Gatún Locks! We will know shortly the exact moment when we will strike!"

Commander Kuttman strode stiffly away. Jaime Coronza, his teeth flashing in a triumphant smile, followed. Jimmy Christopher whirled to the transmitter unit. He shut the metal door; he trimmed the oscillator to the WDC-13 wavelength; he tapped the key swiftly.

Through the night sky, from the submarine-tank streaking through the black waters of the Caribbean, the message flashed into the central Intelligence headquarters in Washington. The whining dot-dash stutter rang in Tim Donovan's ears. He sat motionless, listening, while Z-7 watched him alertly. The boy's eyes widened with consternation as he wrote on a pad. Under his flying pencil words formed:

Sub heading now for Colón Harbor—to leave water and shell Gatún locks—will flash exact moment of attack immediately I learn it—instruct coast artillery batteries at Zone to train guns on land end of West Breakwater—order airplane reconnaissance to spot exact spot when sub leaves water—sub must be

destroyed by artillery fire the instant it emerges or Canal will
be wrecked—strict orders—

Tim Donovan sat motionless when the message ended, staring in horror at the words he had written. He did not move until
Z-7 snapped: "Tim! What is it?" The boy jerked up, his eyes
glistening, and blurted: "I can't give you this message, Chief—I
can't!"

Z-7's jaw-muscles bunched. "We must have it! I have an open
telephone line between this room and General Headquarters.
The Chief of Staff is waiting now to relay orders instantly to
repulse the coming attacks! They can do nothing until we have
Operator 5's word!"

The Washington chief snatched the pad from the boy's trembling hand. With the other, he raised the telephone, but as he
read his motions froze.

"You can't send that, Chief!" Tim Donovan pleaded. "The
coast artillery will blow the sub to pieces—and Jimmy in it!
Jimmy's in it!"

Z-7's eyes smoldered. "Operator 5 knew he would be trapped
inside that sub when our artillery opens on it, but—he did not
hesitate. And—the fate of this nation depends—"

He broke off while Tim Donovan stared transfixed. Slowly
Z-7 lifted the telephone closer to his lips. He snapped
commands which brought the Chief of Staff to the other end
of the line. His voice was husky, breathy, as he spoke.

"Major-General Douglass! Orders just received from Operator 5! Coast Artillery units at the north end of the Canal are
to train their guns now on the edge of the West Breakwater!

The sub-tank will climb onto land there. The instant it appears it must be shelled—destroyed!"

In the receiver, the answer rattled: "We'll follow those orders! We'll blow that damned sub to hell and back!"

Z-7 lowered the telephone in a trembling hand. His face was white and haggard. Tim Donovan stood motionless, peering at him with brimming eyes. Diane Elliot, her red lips parted in horror, found words beyond her. John Christopher's face went ashy as he heard Z-7 speak.

"Tim! Listen for further information from Operator 5. We must know the exact moment when the sub-tank will leave the water! Our shells must stop it instantly when it appears. It will mean—the death of Jimmy Christopher, but—there is nothing else we can do!"

CHAPTER 15
SUICIDE SIGNAL

A BLOOD-RED dawn followed the darkness of terrified tension which paralyzed the United States that night. The crimson light of the rising sun stole across the continent to bring a day of reckoning. It flashed upon the wings of air transports shuttling through the sky—planes carrying precious fuel to points of defense. It glistened on tank-cars speeding from oil-fields previously abandoned as exhausted. It lighted the work of oil-crews laboring feverishly with strange apparatus to draw priceless petroleum from pockets far beneath the crust of the earth. From coast to coast and from border to border, every resource had been brought into play to put the amazing Yerian process to use.

Laboratories hummed, manufacturing the solvent gas, compressing it into tanks; airplanes roared, carrying the tanks to the revivified fields, carrying loads of crude oil back with them to humming refineries. Trucks, trains, bombers, shuttled along the coasts and along the international lines, carrying cargoes of the black gold to supply defenses that had starved for oil. Into the reservoirs of battleships, new power gushed. From the funnels of the merchant marine, fresh, black smoke poured. The sterns of the United States naval vessels once more began cutting the waves, maneuvering to sea to block the approach of the hostile camouflaged fleets of attackers. Into the sky leaped airplanes powered by the newfound fuel.

Through the arteries of a nation, the vital, black life-blood began to flow again!

From Albrook Field and France Field, Canal Zone, pursuit ships leaped into the air, skirting out above a sea made iridescent by the new light of the sun. Above Colón Harbor, swift wings slashed the air; keen-eyed observers watched the end of the West Breakwater through powerful binoculars. With the coming of light, their vigil had begun. Eyes in the sky waited to spot the shells of artillery batteries ready even now to fire.

Somewhere beneath the surface of the sea, the dread *Annihilator* was speeding—closer each minute....

In the steel-walled wireless room, Operator 5 sat tensely at the key. He had remained at his post throughout the night, during the swift passage of the tank-sub beneath the surface. It had approached its mark with amazing speed. It was now nearing the shore. Ringing commands in the voice of Commander Kuttman told Jimmy Christopher that the moment was near when destruction or survival for the United States would be decided....

He tightened when he heard the Commander stride near and declare: "We are ready! The *Annihilator* will leave the water precisely at 8:50. It is only a matter of minutes now! Our guns will rain shells on the Gatún locks even before the American defenses can realize what is happening!"

OPERATOR 5 tensed at the key. *8:50! A matter of minutes!* It was the word for which WDC-13 had been waiting through endless hours—the signal which would forewarn the coast defenses of the Canal Zone of the coming swift attack. Jimmy Christopher's fingertips flexed to the key—and paused.

A quick step sounded outside the door of the wireless room. Across the sill stepped Jaime Coronza. He paused, his black eyes glittering, his teeth shining.

"A signal must be sent now to Commander Jorako in the Pacific—the signal to open fire on the Panamá terminus of the Canal. There is no longer need for code messages. Nothing the United States can do now can stop our attack. I will myself send that signal to Jorako. Move aside, Hinzu!"

Coronza thrust at Operator 5's shoulder. His other hand reached for the sending key. Jimmy Christopher rose tightly as the Spaniard checked the dials. The dark fingers began to tap— and Operator 5's hand snapped to Coronza's wrist. He jerked the spy away from the table, whirled him against the wall.

"Not that message, Coronza!"

The declaration was made—not in the piping tones of Okato Hinzu—but in the ringing voice of Operator 5!

Coronza's face whitened as Jimmy Christopher's hand strayed to the buckle of his belt. A light of dismayed realization burst in the spy's ebon eyes. Instantly, his hand flashed inside his coat—flashed to a weapon held in an armpit holster. And at that instant Operator 5's fingers clicked loose his belt buckle.

Coronza's automatic flashed in the light as swiftly as Jimmy Christopher whipped his supple rapier from its loops and sent the thin sheath flying. The gleaming blade whipped downward with the swiftness of light and Coronza's weapon darted level. Metal sparked against metal as Operator 5 played the steel lash upon the weapon.

A gasp of agony broke from Coronza's thick lips when the razor-edge whipped across the back of his hand, severing tendons that rendered his fingers powerless to move. He willed to pull the trigger of the automatic, yet that finger would not flex. In white-faced fury, he flung himself back against the wall as Operator 5's blade struck magical power against the automatic. The weapon was torn from Coronza's numb fingers and sent whirling through the air.

"Stay back!"

Jimmy Christopher poised the rapier at Coronza's heart. The Spaniard snarled with the fury of an enraged wild animal. He struck out blindly—he leaped! Operator 5 stood motionless, his face drawn, his eyes glittering with midnight darkness. Through the steel of his blade came a tremor. Through the heart of Jaime Coronza, the *épée* plunged, driving out behind, glistening with red. The mad thrust of the spy's attack had driven the steel through his own body.

Operator 5 jerked back, and the crimson-stained rapier flashed up. Jaime Coronza staggered to his knees, clutching at the edge of the table. Beating breath passed through his parted lips as his one trembling hand groped to the sending key. Jimmy Christopher stood grim and cold, making no move, while Coronza struggled to reach the knob—to send a signal to the commander of the hostile fleet outside the Bay of Panamá. A spasm shook his body. He sprawled back. A breathy oath passed his lips. *"Madre de Dios!"* He died....

OPERATOR 5 jerked around, listening alertly through the open door. The hull of the *Annihilator* now was vibrating with a grinding sound. It meant that the tractor treads were biting into the sloping sand of the bottom—that the underwater juggernaut was even then climbing toward the surface. He reached for the sending key. His nimble fingers played it swiftly.

Annihilator appearing 8:50—climbing out now!

He stepped back. He reached for the automatic which Coronza had dropped. He tightened his hand around the butt and leveled it at the transmitting equipment. Swiftly he pulled the trigger. Each explosion rang deafeningly. Each bullet tore into the coils of the transmitter, shattered the tubes, ripped it into snarled wreckage. Until the chamber of the automatic was empty, Operator 5 fired spattering lead to destroy the mechanism.

He spun as swift footfalls sounded beyond. Outside the door, Commander Kuttman came to a rigid stop. His swift glance told him that his sea-monster was left without means of communication—that the gun in the hand of "Hinzu" had silenced it. Operator 5 stood smiling tightly, his empty gun lowered, as Commander Kuttman reached inward. The door slapped shut. A stout bolt clicked.

Within the steel-walled room, Operator 5 stood a prisoner while the turtle of war crawled on its mission of doom.

"ANNIHILATOR APPEARING 8:50! Climbing out now!" In the wireless room of WDC-13, in Washington, Tim Donovan heard the message whine through the ether. His pencil scribbled the words. He stood with bleared eyes, peering at the gaunt-faced Z-7.

"I—I know we've got to destroy the sub, Chief!" he blurted. "Jimmy—Jimmy has just flashed—"

Z-7 snatched the pad from the boy's trembling hand. His face whitened as he jerked up the telephone instrument. He felt that his words would be a sentence of death upon Operator 5. He knew that the waiting artillery of the Canal Zone batteries would blast out destruction a moment after he spoke. His throat tightened as a voice rang in his ears from the far end of the line.

"Yes! What is it? A report? For God's sake—!"

"A report!" Z-7 spoke in agony. "The sub is coming out at 8:50—it is coming out now!"

Over wires leading from the nation's capital, through the ether at the same instant, the warning flashed to the defenses of the Canal Zone. At the great artillery batteries, officers snapped crackling orders. Into the air, to the observers of the scouting planes circling above the northern entrance of the Canal, the same electrifying report rang.

High in the sky, the planes flung themselves into swift circles. Overside, tense observers peered through powerful binoculars. They trained their lenses at the inner end of the West Break-water, holding microphones close to their lips. Seconds dragged past while hearts raced and all the power of a great military reservation waited to strike. Seconds until—

"Sub sighted!"

A FLYING lieutenant snapped the words into his mike as he spotted a dark cloud beneath the water at the end of the West Breakwater. Beneath the surface, a black outline was materi-alizing—the sea-monster. Rapidly it became clearer. Its back broke the swells. Down its sides, over its grinding treads, water streamed. Immediately hatches opened and uniformed men sprang to open others. With amazing swiftness, huge guns reared from the back of the behemoth—guns raised to fling shells into the vital mechanism of the Canal.

Down from the air, the command lightninged into the oper-ations-offices of the coast-defense batteries. Out of the offices, the order flashed to the waiting gun crews. Up behind their case-ments, the great weapons reared. Already aimed, no instant was lost until the command to fire rang and the big guns thundered!

Screaming shells cut swift trajectories across the sky. At the water-line, near the spot where the tremendous *Annihilator* was emerging, power plunged. A shaking geyser of sand and water streaked up; billowing fumes tore away on the wind. A salty rain and a blast of rock-fragments carried through the tearing air. Over the back of the tank-submarine, the force of the shells broke. And as the smoke cleared, the observers in the air peered down to see the black sea-giant crawling deeper into the land.

"Miss! Correction! Five-four!"

"Elevation five-four!"

"Two-three-zero!"

"Two-three-zero!"

"Fire!"

"Fire!"

At the second signal, the huge guns blasted out destruction again. Thunderous concussions shook the earth; screaming shells cut through the sky. Far above, the keen-eyed observers watched. On the back of the *Annihilator* the gun-crews were laboring frantically. Projectiles and charges had been rammed into the breeches. The men were retreating for the firing of the cannon. Over all the world the scream of the falling United States shells carried and hit!

Squarely upon the black back of the monster of doom, the projectiles of the United States guns struck! A blasting explosion tore into the vitals of the submarine. Fire flared over its gleaming length; fumes shrouded it. Through the air and across land, orders flashed again from unit to unit of the Canal defenses.

"The sub has stopped! Keep your range! Fire!"

Again—again—the guns of the Zone blasted furious defiance at the attacking war-engine. Down upon it crashed a wrath of explosive that wrenched the giant machine, that flung it broken into a smoking crater. The forces of destruction crushed it, twisted it, dismembered it. The wind tore at the fumes which blanketed the shore while the observers peered from the sky at a mass of jagged wreckage.

"The tank-sub is destroyed!"

Through air and over wire the triumphant report flashed to Washington.

"The tank-sub is destroyed!"

Into the inner office of WDC-13, the word carried—word which Z-7 and Tim Donovan and Diane Elliot and John Christopher had been awaiting and dreading—news that snatched the color from their faces and darkened their eyes with grief.

"The *Annihilator* is annihilated!"

They spoke no word; they scarcely moved as report after report began to flash into WDC-13. Each one Z-7 received in silence. Each one tightened his grim lips and brought a smouldering new light to his black eyes—yet he read them like a man in a dream.

"United States bombers attacking camouflaged enemy fleet in Bay of Panamá. Four destroyers sinking. Gun attack by ships disrupted! Canal safe!"

And: "Atlantic Fleet steaming to block approach of enemy squadron approaching New York. Certainty that attackers will be kept beyond gun-range of coast. Air corps spotting enemy fleet and preparing to bomb."

"Oil supplies now being rushed to all defense bases, more than adequate to meet needs!"

"The attempted attack upon the United States is crushed!"

Diane Elliot did not even glance at the reports as they were rushed to Z-7's desk. Tim Donovan had turned away, lost in agony. From all points of the nation, information flashed that the United States was removed from danger, that the crisis had passed—but the tough Irish lad had no thought save for Operator 5.

"Jimmy!" broke through his lips wretchedly as he stared into space. "Gee Jimmy! You ordered me to do it—I had to follow orders!"

THE FASTEST available airplane had brought Z-7, with Tim Donovan and Diane Elliot and John Christopher, to Colón. The swiftest automobile had carried them through cleared streets to the military hospital. The message that had started them on their record-breaking journey had been put into their hands long hours after every hostile force threatening the United States had been averted. It had read succinctly:

… OPERATOR 5 REMOVED FROM WRECKED SUBMARINE… GRAVELY INJURED… HOSPITAL-IZED… ASKING FOR YOU… RICHARDS, C.O. ….

Within the quiet hospital room, the four stood crowded around the bed on which Jimmy Christopher lay. His body was swathed in bandages. The tightness of his lips testified that he was suffering agony; yet he smiled. His eyes were drawn with exhaustion, but they shone with a bright fire. He gazed into the faces of the four and said warmly:

"I'm all right now. Seeing you again is better than anything a doctor can do for me. I'll be up and around before you know it. That's a promise!"

Diane's hand was curled warmly around one of his. Tim Donovan was perched on the edge of the bed, grinning broadly, trying to force the tightness from his throat.

"Gee, Jimmy—I don't know what I would have done if—"

"Nor I, Jimmy Christopher," Diane Elliot declared softly. "Don't you ever do a thing like that again! I don't care what happens to the United States—I don't want anything to happen to you!"

Operator 5 smiled. "I knew it was a chance, but there wasn't any other way. The fact the sub was so heavily armored that only big shells could stop it—that meant there was a good chance of coming through. Kuttman's bolting me in that room was actually a protection. It's all over now—there's nothing more to worry about!"

"It's not right," Diane Elliot declared staunchly, "that the country can't know Jimmy did it almost single-handed. He saved more than a hundred million people and the greatest nation in the world—and the people don't even know his name. I want to shout it from the house-tops!"

"But you won't, Di," Operator 5 smiled. "You know that secrecy is absolutely necessary to me. It will always be so. No one must ever know."

JIMMY CHRISTOPHER'S fore finger pressed the button inscribed: *Carleton Victor*. Crowe opened the door of the sumptuous penthouse, bowed. Victor stepped in, glanced about, and smiled.

"I notice, Crowe," he said, "that the apartment is delightfully warm—exactly the right degree."

"Yes, sir," Crowe answered. "You see, sir, I reproached the superintendant again after you had gone. I insisted even more firmly that we must have the proper degree of heat. To put it frankly, sir, I was most severe with him. The result is obvious."

"It is, Crowe. Indeed it is!"

"I regretted that it was necessary, sir," Crowe added, "but for your sake, sir, I made the demand. I am quite sure, sir—because I was so insistent—that we will never again suffer from the cold here."

"Never, Crowe," Victor chuckled. "We are assured of that—quite. Allow me to express my gratitude." He gripped the beaming manservant's thin hand. "Crowe, with all my heart, I thank you!"

POPULAR HERO PULPS AVAILABLE NOW:

THE SPIDER

❏ #1: The Spider Strikes	$13.95
❏ #2: The Wheel of Death	$13.95
❏ #3: Wings of the Black Death	$13.95
❏ #4: City of Flaming Shadows	$13.95
❏ #5: Empire of Doom!	$13.95
❏ #6: Citadel of Hell	$13.95
❏ #7: The Serpent of Destruction	$13.95
❏ #8: The Mad Horde	$13.95
❏ #9: Satan's Death Blast	$13.95
❏ #10: The Corpse Cargo	$13.95
❏ #11: Prince of the Red Looters	$13.95
❏ #12: Reign of the Silver Terror	$13.95
❏ #13: Builders of the Dark Empire	$13.95
❏ #14: Death's Crimson Juggernaut	$13.95
❏ #15: The Red Death Rain	$13.95
❏ #16: The City Destroyer	$13.95
❏ #17: The Pain Emperor	$13.95
❏ #18: The Flame Master	$13.95
❏ #19: Slaves of the Crime Master	$13.95
❏ #20: Reign of the Death Fiddler	$13.95
❏ #21: Hordes of the Red Butcher	$13.95
❏ #22: Dragon Lord of the Underworld	$13.95
❏ #23: Master of the Death-Madness	$13.95
❏ #24: King of the Red Killers	$13.95
❏ **NEW:** #25: Overlord of the Damned	$13.95

THE MYSTERIOUS WU FANG

❏ #1: The Case of the Six Coffins	$12.95
❏ #2: The Case of the Scarlet Feather	$12.95
❏ #3: The Case of the Yellow Mask	$12.95
❏ #4: The Case of the Suicide Tomb	$12.95
❏ #5: The Case of the Green Death	$12.95
❏ #6: The Case of the Black Lotus	$12.95
❏ #7: The Case of the Hidden Scourge	$12.95

G-8 AND HIS BATTLE ACES

❏ #1: The Bat Staffel	$13.95

CAPTAIN SATAN

❏ #1: The Mask of the Damned	$13.95
❏ #2: Parole for the Dead	$13.95
❏ #3: The Dead Man Express	$13.95
❏ #4: A Ghost Rides the Dawn	$13.95
❏ #5: The Ambassador From Hell	$13.95

CAPTAIN ZERO

❏ #1: City of Deadly Sleep	$13.95
❏ #2: The Mark of Zero!	$13.95
❏ #3: The Golden Murder Syndicate	$13.95

OPERATOR 5

❏ #1: The Masked Invasion	$13.95
❏ #2: The Invisible Empire	$13.95
❏ #3: The Yellow Scourge	$13.95
❏ #4: The Melting Death	$13.95
❏ #5: Cavern of the Damned	$13.95
❏ #6: Master of Broken Men	$13.95
❏ #7: Invasion of the Dark Legions	$13.95
❏ #8: The Green Death Mists	$13.95
❏ #9: Legions of Starvation	$13.95
❏ #10: The Red Invader	$13.95
❏ #11: The League of War-Monsters	$13.95
❏ #12: The Army of the Dead	$13.95
❏ #13: March of the Flame Marauders	$13.95

DUSTY AYRES AND HIS BATTLE BIRDS

❏ #1: Black Lightning!	$13.95
❏ #2: Crimson Doom	$13.95
❏ #3: The Purple Tornado	$13.95
❏ #4: The Screaming Eye	$13.95
❏ #5: The Green Thunderbolt	$13.95
❏ #6: The Red Destroyer	$13.95
❏ #7: The White Death	$13.95
❏ #8: The Black Avenger	$13.95
❏ #9: The Silver Typhoon	$13.95
❏ #10: The Troposphere F-S	$13.95
❏ #11: The Blue Cyclone	$13.95
❏ #12: The Tesla Raiders	$13.95

DR. YEN SIN

❏ #1: Mystery of the Dragon's Shadow	$12.95
❏ #2: Mystery of the Golden Skull	$12.95
❏ #3: Mystery of the Singing Mummies	$12.95

MAVERICKS

❏ #1: Five Against the Law	$12.95
❏ #2: Mesquite Manhunters	$12.95
❏ #3: Bait for the Lobo Pack	$12.95
❏ #4: Doc Grimson's Outlaw Posse	$12.95
❏ #5: Charlie Parr's Gunsmoke Cure	$12.95